BLOOD FEUD

BLOOD FEUD

by Rosemary Sutcliff

E. P. DUTTON   NEW YORK

To all those who answered the author's distress
signals, and without whose help and advice this
book would never have got written at all.

The maps in this book have been redrawn by Laurence
Fullbrooke from maps in Dimitri Obolensky's *The
Byzantine Commonwealth*, Weidenfeld & Nicolson, 1971,
and the source material is used by kind permission of
the publishers.

First published in the U.S.A. 1977 by E. P. Dutton

Library of Congress Cataloging in Publication Data

Sutcliff, Rosemary   Blood feud

SUMMARY: Sold into slavery to the Northmen in the tenth
century, a young Englishman becomes involved in a blood
feud which leads him to Constantinople and a totally
different way of life.

[1. Northmen—Fiction. 2. Istanbul—History—Fiction]
I. Title
PZ7.S966Bl   [Fic]   76-58502   ISBN 0-525-26730-1

Printed in the U.S.A.
10 9 8 7 6 5 4 3 2

Contents

Maps appear on pages vi-vii and 146-147.

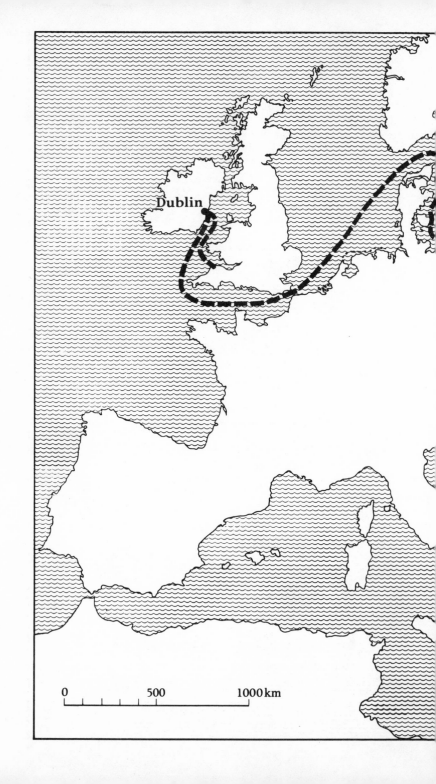

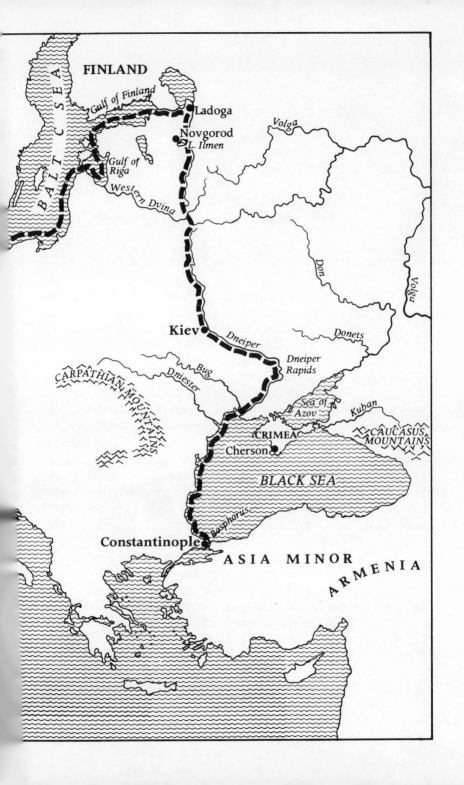

Historical Note

When one thinks of the Northmen, the Vikings, one generally thinks of them following the seaways westward, raiding the coasts of Britain, colonizing Orkney and Iceland and Greenland, maybe even reaching America. One does not think so much of the other great Viking thrust, south-eastward—the men of Sweden and the Baltic shores of Denmark forcing their way along the vast rivers that link the Baltic with the Black Sea, to Constantinople, and on to carry their trade and sometimes their dreaded raven war-banners the length and breadth of the Mediterranean. Yet this south-eastward thrust of the Viking Kind, sometimes in the peaceful ways of trade, sometimes as a fighting aristocracy, the trading posts and settlements they founded as they went along (which presently became cities such as Novgorod and later Kiev), the gradual mingling of their own blood with that of the wandering Slav tribes who were there before them—all these were the beginning of Russia, more than twelve hundred years ago.

Khan Vladimir, Prince of Kiev, was a real person, one of the first rulers of what was beginning to be a nation; he was later made a saint for bringing his people to Christianity (but why he did not bring them to the Muhammadan faith instead, you will know when you have read this story). He really did, for an agreed price, lead his six thousand Vikings down to Constantinople, to help the sorely-pressed Emperor of Byzantium Basil II deal with rebellion at home and an enemy on his frontiers, in the year 987 A.D. And it was some of these six thousand, remaining behind when the rest went north again, who became the famous Varangian Guard, the Emperor's bodyguard, serving him and his successors until the last of them—by that time they were mostly English—died at their posts when Constantinople fell to the Turks almost six hundred years later.

All the big background events and the big background people of this book are real. But the small foreground people, Jestyn Englishman who tells the story, Thormod Sitricson and Anders and Herulf, Hakon Ship-Chief, and Demetriades the Physician, fat Cloe and the Lady Alexia and the rest are all of my making; and so is the blood feud which in one way or another bound them together.

1 Wind from the West

In the lengthening spring evenings the light lingers behind the dome of St. Mary Varangarica, St. Mary of the Barbarians, long after the lanterns are pricking out among the shipping and along the crowded wharves and jetties of the Golden Horn. It is a sight that I never tire of, when life spares me time for looking at it: the clear green twilight over the roofs of Constantinople.

Then Alexia brings the candles. It is a task she never leaves to our daughter, or to the house slaves. And the spring twilight beyond the window deepens into full dusk, and this small crowded study at the top of the house warms out of the shadows, so that when she has gone again, I can see it twice over—once in reality, once by its disjointed reflection in the glass window-panes: the cherished books on the shelves, the locked cabinet where I keep my most precious or most dangerous drugs, the white oleander in its painted pot, newly broken from bud into flower. In the window glass, too, I can see myself, as though I looked at another man sitting at the table with its litter of books and specimens and writing materials—there is always so much to learn, so much to record, so many notes to take. A big man, I suppose, lean and rangy and scarred as an old hound, with a mane of hair brindled grey and yellow. Jestyn the Englishman, so most men call me, though indeed I am but half Saxon and half of an older breed.

Alexia always brings the candles a little too soon. Maybe she is afraid that I shall be trying to work without enough light to see by. Maybe she is afraid that in the dusk I shall start remembering and

grow home-hungry. It is true that dusk is a good time for remembering, and of all times a spring twilight is apt to turn the heart
homeward. And I do remember so many things, small unimportant
things: gorse, honey-scented along the headlands, and the crash
and cream of the long sea rollers beating on the jagged Western
coast, curlew crying over the high moors, the smell of a new-born
calf brought in from the herd. But I have learned, as Alexia, born
and bred under these skies, has not had to learn it, that Home is
not Place but People. Kinships, the ties that we make as we go
along. My ties are with her, here in this tall crumbling house in
the Street of the Golden Mulberry Tree, in a shallow scooped-out
grave in the Thracian hills, among the poor folk in the hospital
where much of my work is done. I have no ties, no kinships in the
land where I was a boy. I do remember, but without any longing
to go back over the road.

My father was a wandering smith out of the far south-western horn
of Britain, where the folk claim no kinship with the Saxon kind,
but are of the older breed I spoke of. Smithing is a fine trade for a
man with wandering in his feet, and a smith is sure of work and
welcome wherever he goes. My mother was a Saxon farmer's
daughter who left her own folk to follow him when he went back
into the west again. So I was born in a village of the high moors
far over beyond the Tamar River. And my first memory is of
squatting in the sun-warm dust before my father's smithy, playing
with the little clay horse daubed with ochre spots that was the
darling of my heart, and hearing the ding of my father's hammer
on the anvil; and of my mother coming out from the living-place
behind the smithy, and scooping me up, saying, 'Come, Baba, it
is time for sleep.'

Why that evening above any other, I'd not be knowing, but it
was that evening I noticed for the first time that she spoke to me
in a tongue she used to no one else, and that no one else in the
village used at all. I thought for years that it was some kind of
private language that was for me because she loved me, until I
came to understand that it was the Saxon tongue. Why, I have
never known; maybe it was for some kind of last link with her own
world and her own people. At all events it has stood me in good
stead, for I have needed both tongues in my time, and when I

needed a third, I found it easier, I think, to learn that also, than a child who has been reared speaking only one.

When I was five summers old, my father was kicked by a horse that he was shoeing, and died of the hurt. Then my mother might have taken me and gone back to her own world. But maybe her own world would not have taken her back; and one of the Chieftain's hearth-companions had looked long in her direction, and so she went to him instead. I grew up under my stepfather's roof, and ran with the hounds and the pigs, and joined the other boys scaring the birds from the newly-sown barley, and began to take a hand with the cattle as I grew older.

My stepfather must have hoped that my mother would have other children for him, but she never did, and I think, for that, he hated me. He was not cruel to me, but on the night she died, while she lay in the house-place with her hair combed and her hands folded, and the candles burning at her head and feet, he opened the house-place door and said to me, 'The door is open.'

And I walked out through it and away. And did not see the priest come to sign her with the cross and speak the prayers for her soul. I was just twelve years old.

Like enough, I could have found shelter with someone else in the village, if I had asked for it. But I did not think of that. I was not thinking very clearly of anything at all; and maybe the wandering that had been in my father's feet was in mine also. It was getting near to dawn, and there was nothing and no one to wait for, so I started walking.

The dark was paling to ash grey as I came down to the old trading track that ran below the village, and a soft buffeting wind from the west was combing the white-tufted moor-grass all one way; there was beginning to be a thin flurry of rain, and I turned eastward along the track, simply for the sake of having it behind me.

I have wondered, since, what shape my life would have taken if the wind had been blowing from the east, in that grey dawn.

Later, I came to a place where the track forked, and took the left-hand branch for the very good reason that, at least on that first stretch, it led downhill. My memory of the days that followed is blurred, as though I looked back through a moorland mist. For the most part, I must have lived off the country, though it was growing late in the year for birds' eggs. Once or twice I think I begged from a woman at a steading gate; once I know I helped a man droving cattle, whose dog had gone lame, and shared his supper and his fire at the day's end. And then one day, towards evening, I came, with the shoes worn off my feet, round the shoulder of a wooded ridge, and saw—away to my left—a narrow combe running down to something shimmering sword-grey between two juts of land, that I knew from listening to the tales of travelling men must be the sea.

I headed towards it, and lost it as I dropped downhill. Instead, the combe widened before me. Behind me were the high moors and the wild wind-stunted oak woods; below, I saw rough pasture that men had in-taken from the wilds; and in the small fields across the valley, below the turf-and-thatch huddle of a village, they were getting in the harvest. I stood looking across to the homely pattern of fields, and knew suddenly that I was tired and hungry. It was the first time I had thought clearly about anything since the night my mother died. I thought, 'It may be that in this place they will give me work and food and a night's shelter,' and I walked on downhill, forded the little stream at the bottom where it ran bright and shallow over speckled stones, and came up the far side to the in-fields, where the men were cutting the last swathes of the evening.

I checked among the hawthorns of a wind-break, and stood looking on, wishing that I had been there earlier, when the women would have been bringing out the great noon-time jars of buttermilk to set in the shade. And as I stood there, I heard a low growl behind me, and swung round, to see a man with a couple of leashed deerhounds standing not a spear's length away. He stood leaning on his hunting spear and looking down at me. He was hard-faced and weather-beaten, and wore a rough woollen tunic like any of the men in the fields; but it was strapped round his waist by a belt of fine crimson leather, and by this, and by the fact that he walked abroad with his hounds while everyone else slaved at the harvest, I guessed that he must be the chief. A Thane, my mother would have called him.

I made the sign for coming in peace, with open hands to show that there were no weapons in them; and he grinned. 'You ease my mind. For if you had been the leader of a war-band in disguise, surely we should all have had cause to tremble in our shoes!

Where are you from, skinned rabbit?' He spoke in the Saxon tongue, and I knew that I had come back into my mother's world.

'From further west,' I said, too weary even to resent the jibe. 'Along the trade road.'

'And where do you go?'

I hunched a shoulder. 'I do not know.'

'Alone?'

'Aye.'

'You haven't the look of a wandering beggar-cub. Have you run away from your village?'

It is ill-mannered to ask such questions of a stranger before he has eaten; at any rate of a grown man, but I was only twelve, and anyway I was past caring. I wanted food and shelter and I was most likely to get it if I told the man with the deerhounds what he wanted to know. 'My mother died, and there was no place for me in the hut of the man she was wedded to.'

'And so you went on your travels. Is it in your mind to spend your life wandering up and down the world claiming Guest-Right at every hall you come to?'

'I can work,' I said. 'I can set my hand to most things, and I'm good with cattle.'

'Are you so? Well, come you up to the village with the rest. Food and shelter for the night, you shall have; and in the morning it may be that we will see as to this cattle skill of yours.' And with his hounds at heel, he went on, up towards the village, where the bracken-thatched roof of the Hall rose whale-backed among the clustering bothies.

So that night I ate my fill of kale broth and cheese and barley bannock, squatting in the Guest Place nearest to the door of the Chief's Fire Hall, and slept warm between the peat stack and the pig-pen hurdles. And next morning I was shaken into wakefulness by a man with a small red angry eye, who demanded if I meant to sleep all day while the cattle waited.

That was my first encounter with old Gyrth the cattle-herd, who was to be my master for the next five years.

2 The Shore-Killing

I was quite happy, in the five years that I spent with Gyrth. I made no friends; that was nothing new, for I had always been something of a lone wolf. But I had the cattle and I had the two big savage cattle-dogs, above all, the bitch, Brindle. I got into the way of talking to Brindle in the British tongue, as my mother had talked to me in the Saxon; and I suppose for the same reason. The life was hard, and there were bad times in it: the winter nights spent hunting for a strayed cow; the feast days when as soon as our prayers were said in the little wattle church, and the merrymaking began, Gyrth got drunk and beat me—though before I was fifteen, the beatings came to an end because by then I was taller and stronger than he was. But there were the good times too: long lazy days spent lying up among the furze on the headlands above a crooning summer sea, with Brindle beside me alert for any beast that strayed from the slow-grazing drift of the herd, and a kestrel hovering high overhead; calving time, and the little leggy calves still wet from their birth to be lifted up to the cows' flanks and coaxed to suck. The only time I ever knew Gyrth gentle was in the calving season, especially with a cow in trouble and needing help to bring her calf into the world. He was the best cattleman and the best cattle doctor in five manors; and if he beat me, he also taught me his skills; and something more, for it was working with him at such times that I learned a thing about myself which it was good that I should know, though I did not understand it for years afterwards.

And then my time with Gyrth and the cattle was over.

One evening a storm blew up. It was no greater than others of the late summer gales along that black-fanged coast, that send ships running for shelter where little enough shelter is to be found. But it struck without warning, out of a clear sky. There had been a soft offshore breeze all day, warm with the scents of bracken and bog myrtle; then almost between gust and gust, it shifted, and changed and began to blow low along the ground, brushing up the leaves of the thorn trees to a rough silver; and in a little, the sky was covered by a thin membrane of cloud, like the skin of warm milk, and there began to be a hollow sounding of the sea. But even Gyrth, who was as weatherwise as most of his kind, did not guess how soon the storm would be upon us. He sniffed the wind like a hound and squinted at the sky. 'Going to be a bit of a blow before morning. Rain too, I'd not wonder. Best take Brindle and get the yearlings down off Black Head.'

I whistled the old bitch after me, and set off; but before I was half-way up to Black Head, the wind was roaring through the oak woods, the sky racing with darkly huddled cloud like flocks of driven sheep; and by the time I came out on to the open Head above its deep sea inlet, fine grey swathes of rain were driving in from the west, cutting sight to a couple of spear throws. Most of the yearlings were bunched in the lea of the outcrop of dark rocks that gave the place its name; but three or four were lacking. Most like, I thought, they had drifted on down the lea slope before the wind. I left Brindle to keep the rest together, and pushed on after the strays.

They were widely scattered, and the sodden daylight was fading into the dusk before I had them all gathered up; and it was the edge of dark when I got them back to the rest. They were still huddled in the shelter of the outcrop, with Brindle watchfully in charge. She wagged her tail in greeting when I came out of the murk, and I spared a moment to fondle her great rough head and praise her. 'So, so, that was well done, my girl. Home now.'

She gathered the cattle as she had been taught, and together we began the homeward drove, down the windward slope and over toward the combe head and the herd and gleam of firelight from the doorway of Gyrth's bothy.

But we never got there.

Only as far as the place where a rough path, half lost among rocks and long sea grasses, left the track we were following and plunged over the cliff edge down to the inlet below. The rain seemed to blow aside like a curtain just as we got there, and for a moment I had a clear view of the cove, and a flickering blur of light among the rocks that made me check and peer down. Someone had lit a fire down there on the shingle, where the long jagged comb of rock running seaward gave shelter from the pounding waves. There was always driftwood to be found among the boulders and sea—fretted crannies of the cliff foot that would be dry from the rain. There was something else down there too, that had not been there earlier: a long slim shape of darkness on the paler shingle. I peered down through the wind and rain, and realized that it was a ship. Some ship that had come running for shelter before the storm, and either by luck or superb seamanship, was now beached safe in the lea of the rocks above the boiling tideline.

Merchantman or raider? It could be the same thing at times, for many a trading vessel of the Northmen turned riever on the way home from an unsuccessful voyage, or when they themselves had met with raiders and lost their cargo.

My heart began to race, and something within me shouted 'Danger!' as I pulled back from the cliff edge and turned in frantic haste to get the cattle away. But it was too late. We hadn't pushed on another spear throw, Brindle weaving to and fro at the heels of the jostling yearlings, when all at once the darkness among the wind-lashed furze bushes was alive with men.

Maybe there were no more than six or eight, but in the stormy darkness they might have been an army. The world burst into a reeling chaos of shouting men and bellowing cattle. The yearlings were all ways at once. It did not last long. I pulled my knife from my belt and went for a big man who loomed suddenly before me. My foot slipped on the sodden turf, and naked steel went whitt-t-t past my ear as I pitched down. In all likelihood that fall saved my life. I had a moment's confused awareness of men and cattle above and all around me, and of Brindle springing with a snarl at the throat of one of the raiders; and then a flying hoof caught me on the side of the head, there was a burst of bright sparks inside my skull, and I went out into jagged darkness.

When I came back to myself, the rain had stopped, and I was

sprawled on my back staring up at a blurred moon riding high in a sky of racing cloud-wrack. I lay for a while vaguely wondering where I was, and why my head hurt so much, until suddenly the memory of what had happened kicked me in the belly. I rolled on to my face and vomited, then got slowly on to one elbow and clawed myself up to my knees.

Under the booming of the wind and the surf, there was silence all about me. Nothing moved but the lashing furze branches: no men, no cattle. I managed to get up, the world dipping and swimming round me; and with my first step fell over something that brought me to my knees again. It was the body of old Brindle. I put out my hand and felt a sodden mass of hair with no life under it; and my hand came away sticky from the gaping hole in her throat. I wiped it on the grass. And as I did so, a kind of red wave rose from somewhere deep within me, engulfing all things save the thirst to kill.

In the years since then, I have come to know how large a part the blow on my head must have played in what followed after. Such a blow may make a man seem quite foolish, or see two of everything and wish only to sleep; or be for hours, maybe days, as though he were fighting drunk.

I felt about and found my knife, then got once more to my feet, and stumbled back to the place where I had first seen the fire in the cove. It was still there, and the long ship-shadow beyond it, and a movement of figures, half seen in the flame-light. They would not care who saw their blaze, I thought, for when the Viking Kind come ashore, sensible folk stay away. It seemed to me that I was thinking quite clearly, and yet I did not think it at all foolish that I should be scrambling down the cliff path towards them, with a knife in my hand. They had killed my dog, the only thing I had to love, and I was going to kill as many of them as I could, in return.

I slipped and half fell the last part of the way, picked myself up, knife still in hand, and charged on towards the dark figures round the fire. I was seeing everything through a red haze, but sharp-edged and for one instant frozen into stillness like a picture on a wall: the battered ship, the wind-torn fire, the carcasses of three yearlings lying on the blood-stained shingle while great joints hacked from them were already half-cooking, half-scorching on spear points over the heart of the blaze, the men in rough dark seamen's clothes, their faces all turned towards me as I ran.

Why they did not kill me then, I shall never know. A flung spear would have brought me down easily enough. Maybe, seeing that I was alone, it seemed scarce worth the trouble at least until they had had a bit of fun with me first.

Then I was among them, and the scene splintered out of its stillness. Someone stepped into my path, grinning. I saw the white animal flash of teeth in a wind-burned face, and the firelight on the blade of a dirk, and hurled myself forward, choking with the rage and grief that was in me. 'You killed my dog! Devils! You killed my dog!' There was a blare of laughter, and an arm came round me from behind, crushing me back against somebody's body. My dagger hand was caught and wrenched upward. I fought like a trapped animal, and when the knife was twisted from my grasp, ducked my head and bit into the arm that held me. I tasted blood between my teeth, and the laughter turned to a bellow of surprise and pain, but the grip never slackened.

'Ach! It bites like a wolf-cub!' somebody said. The Norse is kin to the Saxon tongue, and even through the red haze, I could understand after a fashion.

'It's the herdboy. Didn't you kill it, then?'

'Seems not. But that's a matter easy to set right.'

'You killed my dog!' I yelled again.

'It gives tongue like a wolf-cub, too.'

The grip shifted, a giant of a man loomed up in front of me, and the point of a dagger was tickling my throat. 'So now we kill you too, and that will make all neat and ship-shape,' he said gravely. The rest crowded round, laughing. I had ceased to struggle, and stood still, knowing—but as though I were standing aside and knowing it of somebody else—that in a few more breaths I should be dead.

But another man, who seemed to be the chief, struck the dagger aside. 'Leave that.'

The giant turned on him, showing his teeth a little, but lowering his dagger-hand nonetheless. 'Why? Is he a long lost brother of yours?'

'Do not you be a fool, Aslak; what use is he to us dead? We can't eat him as we can the cattle—'

'There's not a good mouthful on his bones anyway,' someone guffawed, 'and wolf meat's too strong for my stomach.'

'And alive, he'll fetch his price in the Dublin Slave Market. We haven't done so well, this trip, that we can afford to toss aside a bit of easy profit that falls into our hands.'

There was a general growl of agreement; and the giant with the dagger shrugged, half laughing, and thrust the blade back into his belt.

'Tie him up and dump him against the rocks yonder, out of the way.' The man who seemed to be their chief jerked his thumb towards the sheltering outcrop.

So they bound my ankles together, and lashed my wrists behind me, with cords that somebody brought from the boat; and hauled me over to the rocks and flung me down there like a calf for branding; and went back to their own affairs.

Everything had begun to go far off and hazy; and I knew very little more, until suddenly—it must have been a good while later— the meat was cooked, and somebody was jabbing a sizzling lump of it against my mouth on the point of a dagger, shouting, 'Eat! If we do not kill you, eat!'

The chief nodded, grinning from ear to ear, with a lump of fat hanging half out of his mouth. 'It is you—your people that give the meat; now it is fair that you feast with the rest of us.'

And a third man struck in: 'A good host should always set his guests at their ease by eating with them himself.'

'And since no other one of your people seems coming to join the feast. . . .'

'I am thinking it's not often you fill your belly full of the good red beef you herd for them.'

And that was true enough; and the lump of meat was still jabbing against my teeth. And I opened my mouth and ate.

Not because I was afraid they would kill me if I did not, but for a mingling of reasons that went deeper than that. I thought what did I owe to my mother's kind? And what did it matter? What did anything matter? Old Brindle was dead.

So I ate the meat, and knew, even as I did so, that now I could never go back to the world that was only just behind me. Even if I were not, in all likelihood, going to be killed, even if I were not back. I had broken the Tabu, the unwritten Law of the Spirit, that binds all herdsmen, eaten the stolen flesh of the cattle I herded; I had done the Forbidden Thing. I threw most of it up again soon after, but that was merely the blow on my head. I had done the Forbidden Thing, and there could be no going back.

I ate, and threw up, and slept. And when I woke, still with a splitting head, it was morning, and the seas had gentled, and the men were running their ship down into the surf.

They stowed the uneaten meat below the thwarts, and myself along with it. They had slackened off my ankle ropes and rebound my hands in front of me. (Every cattleman knows that the better the condition of his steers when they come to market, the better price they will fetch.)

So, they pushed out into the shallows; and lying among the cargo bales and the meat, I looked up past the swinging backs of the rowers, and saw against the drifting sky, and the cliff tops sinking astern, the dark figure of the Ship-Chief standing braced at the steering oar. I heard his rhythmic shout—'*Lift* her! *Lift* her!'—and felt for the first time the liveness of a ship beneath me, lifting and twisting and dipping into the long swell of the Western seas.

The red haze of my rage had left me, and I felt cold and sick, and empty of all things. I could not even grieve for old Brindle any more. It all seemed so long ago.

3 The Viking Breed

Dublin is a fine town. And through its streets the Danes and Northmen ruffle up and down like fighting-cocks, rubbing shoulders and picking quarrels with Saracens from Spain and merchants of Venice and the Frankish lands. It was the first and finest of the Norse settlements in Ireland, so I have heard, though when I was there it still had to pay tribute to King Malachy in his high Hall at Tara. But for the first few days, all I saw of the town was the open sheds down by the ship-strand, where the slaves were housed and the merchants who were interested in such goods came to buy.

Sometimes a ship's crew with a full cargo of thralls to sell would handle the business themselves, but with only one or two, it was simpler to sell to one of the dealers, though of course the price was lower that way. So I was passed over to a middleman, who had a thrall-ring riveted on to my neck, and kept me in the back of the slave-shed for a few days, until the cut on my head had near enough finished healing. After that he brought me out front, and tethered me with a few others of my kind, on show to the passers-by.

I was still in the same state of cold emptiness, and everything and everyone around me seemed not quite real; and only one of my fellows comes to my mind with any clearness. And that, maybe, was only because he was the one tethered next to me. A huge man with a simple face, who told me that he came from Bristow town, and that his folk were poor, so that his father had had to sell either him or the cow. He seemed quite resigned, and sat with his arms across his knees, staring out at the shipping along the keel strand, and the grey waters of the bay.

Soon after noon, a trader came along the slave-sheds, picking out this one and that, to complete a cargo that he was shipping up to Orkney for the Jarl's private purchase. We all knew that while he was yet afar off, for he had a loud voice, and there was always a stillness along the slave-sheds when a possible buyer came past. He picked out the Bristow man, and there was the usual haggling over the price.

'He's not much more than a mazelin. I could get a man with all his wits for that.'

'Look at his shoulders! That man could pull a plough as well as any ox, and does an ox need wits, so long as he has a man behind him with a whip?'

But the amount was agreed at last, and the man led away by a rope slipped through his thrall-ring. He looked back once, but the merchant's man jerked the rope, and they disappeared into the crowd.

I never knew his name, and I never saw him again.

My own turn came next day.

I had squatted there so long, while buyers came and went along the open space before the slave-sheds, that I had passed into a kind of dream of passing feet—nothing else, just the feet—and when another knot of them came by, mostly in some kind of deer-skin boots or raw-hide shoes and leggings, I did not bother to look up. Not until they ambled to a halt, and the shadows of their owners, long in the evening sunlight, fell across me.

'What about this one?' said a voice.

I looked up then; and saw the reason for a certain jinking and chiming of metal that had come with them. The men who stood there glancing me over, were of the true Viking Kind that I had heard of in stories and been told to pray God I might never see in life. Men with grey ring-mail strengthening their leather byrnies, iron-bound war-caps, long straight swords. One had a silver arm-ring, one had studs of coral in the clasp of his belt, one wore a rough wolfskin cloak.

'I still don't see why we want a thrall, anyway,' said the one with the arm-ring.

Another laughed. A man with a fierce narrow face and a sprig of late bell-heather thrust into the neck-buckle of his byrnie. 'Because I am aweary of cleaning my own gear.'

'And what do we do with him when the time comes for heading homeward in the spring?'

'Sell him off again.'

The merchant had appeared from somewhere, and his man kicked me to my feet. 'Up, you.'

I doubt if either of them had much hope of a sale; the Northmen had the look of men just passing an idle hour. But there was always the chance, and you don't make a fortune by letting even the slimmest chances go whistling down the wind.

The man with the arm-ring shrugged. 'How much do you want for him?'

'Twelve gold pieces.'

'You're jesting, of course; we could buy a good pony for that.'

The dealer hunched his shoulders to his ears. 'Then go you and buy a pony. I thought it was a thrall your honours wanted.'

'Seven gold pieces,' said another of the Northmen, leaning against the corner-post.

'Now it is you who jest.'

'Na na, no jest. But now that I look at the dunt in his head. . . .' He glanced round at the rest. 'Let's be getting on. It's never worth while buying damaged goods.'

'What!' protested the dealer. 'That little scathe he got when he was taken? Why, in a month, you'll not be able to run your thumb-nail along the scar.'

'Tell that to the sea-mews.'

'Eight gold pieces,' said the man in the wolfskin, suddenly.

It was the first time he had spoken, and something in his voice, a level voice but very alive and with a hint of laughter, reached me through the daze in which I was still living, so that I looked round quickly, and saw him, real among all the rest who were only shadows. A man not more than two or three years older than myself, somewhat short for a Northman, with his head held on a strong neck above shoulders that were too broad for his height; eyes as grey as a sword blade, thick russet brows that almost met above his nose, a mouth that matched his voice—wide and straight, with laughter quirking at the corners.

I suppose it was not a particularly memorable face, but it was the first to seem real to me in a long while; and I have remembered it well enough for more than half a lifetime.

'Don't be a fool, Thormod,' said he of the arm-ring. 'We don't need a thrall. If we want to waste all that gold, there are more interesting ways of doing it.'

Nobody paid any heed to him.

'I-want a thrall,' said the man Thormod. Our eyes met and held.

'Ten,' said the dealer. 'I shall lose by it, but it's getting late in the season, and I'd not grieve to have him off my hands. Ten gold pieces, and that's my last word.'

'Nine,' said Thormod.

The man leaning against the corner-post pushed off impatiently. 'Leave it, Thormod, we've wasted enough time here.'

'I have not,' said Thormod.

'Nine then, and may your soul rot!' Somehow it had ceased to have to do with the rest of the band, and become a matter between the dealer and the man in the wolfskin cloak. Thormod had pulled a slim leather pouch from the breast of his byrnie, and was shaking it out into the palm of the dealer's hand. Watching, I saw a shower of silver and bronze, and the glint of gold. But not enough gold. Surely not nearly enough gold. . . .

But Thormod laughed, and turned to the man with the flower in his neck-buckle. 'Haki, how much have you in your pouch?'

'Three gold pieces,' said Haki. 'I do not have to look; I know it all too well.'

'Lend me two of them, and I'll lend you my shield-thrall to clean your gear.'

'See that you do, then.' Haki felt inside his own byrnie, produced the two gold pieces, and tossed them across to Thormod, who caught them and tossed them up and caught them again.

'You're a shipmate worth the name! We're still short—what about you, Eric? Tostig? No? Stinking fish, the lot of you!'

'Three gold pieces short,' agreed the dealer. 'And I've not all evening to waste, my young Lordlings, if you have.'

I felt coldly sick. If the man in the wolfskin cloak left me here. . . . I think I made some kind of panic movement, and again his eyes met mine.

'Did I deny it? Wait, and you shall have the rest.'

One-handed, still holding the gold in the other, he freed the heavy silver brooch at the shoulder of his cloak, swung the heavy wolfskin free, and dropped it at the dealer's feet. 'There. It's a good cloak, almost new, and the brooch alone must be worth upward of a gold piece.' And he tossed the money down on top of it.

'And what,' demanded the man he had called Tostig, 'will you do this winter, when the wind blows down off the mountains?'

'Shiver,' said Thormod cheerfully.

And so, as though half in jest, after a little more haggling I was bought for six gold pieces and a wolfskin cloak; and became shield-thrall to Thormod Sitricson of the Dublin Garrison.

4 The Amber Talisman

The Viking Garrison of Dublin in those days—and like enough it's the same today—were a motley and ever-changing pack. Some were men who had settled; who had made their home there, with their women and children in the town. But others were adventurers; men who had made their own land too hot for comfort; younger sons following wherever their swords led them. Sometimes a whole ship's crew, taking service for a few months or a few years, their ships waiting in the boat-sheds until the next spring, or the spring after, should wake the old Viking fever in them once again.

They had their living quarters in the huddle of turf bothies behind the old King's Palace, they and their ponies and their hounds, the thralls and on-hangers and camp women that they had gathered to them. It was like a kind of rough and ready town-within-a-town, with here and there a woman spinning in a door-way, and here and there a hound scratching for fleas; a wolfskin hung up to dry on a stand of crossed spears; and pigs and gulls alike scavenging among the garbage heaps.

Thormod and Haki and Tostig and Eric, all members of the same ship's crew, shared one of the turf-rooted sleeping bothies between them. And my sleeping-place—tethered like a hound for the first few nights—was on a rug across the door-hole. I was Thormod's shield-thrall, but Thormod was generous with his property, and so I was at the beck and call of all the rest as well. I did not greatly care. For a slave, lacking freedom in any case, it makes little difference whether he cleans armour and fetches beer for one man or four. Yet the knowledge that of the four, it was Thormod I belonged to, had a certain meaning for me, nonetheless.

As time passed, and the evenings shortened and the wild geese came down from the north at the nearing of winter, I began to know something of the strange half-Irish, half-Viking city. For speaking the British tongue, I could understand the Irish folk after a fashion, and make myself understood in return; and so almost wherever they went, Thormod and his mates got into the way of taking me with them. It was easier to have me to talk for them and tell them what other men said, than to try to learn the Irish speech themselves. I came to know the boat-sheds along the strand, where the long slim vessels, the *Sea Swallow* among them, waited like horses in their stables, for springtime to set them on the seaways again. The markets where the merchants and seamen of all the world met and chaffered over hides and corn and copper, and lumps of raw yellow amber from the Baltic, and hunting dogs and slaves. I came to know the narrow ways snaking between the huddled bothies that were some turf-and-timber built, some still roofed with spars and ships' awnings; I knew, from the outside, the church of St. Columba with its gable-end cross stark against the sky—for Cuiran the King was Christian and his city Christian, after a fashion, with him, though many of the Viking Kind still made their vows on Thor's Ring in the little dark God-House with the blood-splashed doorposts, beyond the boat-strand. I knew the King's timbered and painted Hall amid its byres and barns and outbuildings; and every ale-house and wine-shop in the sprawling length and breadth of the city.

But they did not always take me with them. I was not with them when they strolled down into the town in search of amusement on Midwinter's night—Christmas night—Yule. I had been to get myself some supper—there was always food for all comers, thrall or free, to be had from the cookshed behind the King's Hall— and with a good meal of bannock and ewe-milk cheese inside me, I had come back and made up the fire on the bothy's small central hearth, and settled to clearing up and tending the war-gear that they had left scattered when they came off duty. I mind sitting with Thormod's war-cap on my knees, burnishing the iron rim; and hearing, behind the rub of the burnishing cloth and the flutter of the hearth flames and the quiet of the empty bothy, the surf-roar of Dublin keeping its Midwinter Festival.

Last year, we had lit the Midwinter Fires on the thorn-crowned hillock above the village as usual, to the fury, every year the same fury, of Aldred the Priest, who had every year the same things to say as to the lighting of pagan fires by his Christian flock, to help the Sun grow strong and bring the summer back. This year, too, the fire would be blazing, and Priest Aldred in the same fury, poor old man. And suddenly, achingly, I wondered where I would be, whose thrall I would be, the next time the Midwinter Fires were lit.

'What will you do with him when the time comes for heading homeward in the spring?' Tostig had asked, that first day down at the slave-sheds; and Haki had said, 'Sell him off again.' And come the spring and the seafaring weather, they would run the *Sea Swallow* down into the water and head for home. And for me, there would be the slave-sheds again, and a new master. The thought brought me up with a sickening jerk. Thormod was not a particularly kind master, but I had never known much of kindness, and it did not greatly matter to me. After that moment at the slave-sheds when I had thought that he looked at me as a man looks at a man, he had whistled me to heel like a hound; and like a hound, I had followed. Still, I knew that I could live as a thrall so long as I was Thormod's, but to be anybody else's would be beyond bearing.

I turned my thinking hurriedly aside, and reached for Thormod's worn leather byrnie that lay across the foot of the sleeping-place. As I picked it up, something that had been caught inside it fell out. A lump of raw yellow amber, roughly hammer-head shaped, with a hole in one end, and trailing through the hole, a broken leather thong. I had seen it often round his neck, when he stripped off to sleep, or to scrub away the muck and stiffness of a day's hunting. He always wore it inside his sark; so it must be that he wore it not for ornament, but for luck or for some private reason of his own; maybe for its shape. Many of the Northmen wore Thor's Hammer carved in bone or hammered out of metal round their necks for a kind of talisman I knew, and this, being natural, would be all the more a thing of power. And I had never seen it off his neck until now. The thong must have worn thin, and somehow he must have caught it when he pulled off his war-gear.

I sat turning the thing over in my hand and looking at it in the light of the fire. It was the colour of honey that runs from the comb; almost clear in places, so that the firelight shone through it, clouded with a kind of milky shadow at one end, like the ghost of a fern frond caught in the liquid gold. It was beautiful; and as I sat holding it in my hands, it grew warm, and seemed to give off a curious feeling of liveness, after the way of amber, which never forgets that it was once the sun-warm tears of a living tree.

I remember thinking, 'This thing has power! Surely it has power of some sort! And if he misses it in the midst of such a night, he will not know where he lost it. And if he does not miss it, then it may be that without it, harm will come to him.' That was a thought that would have angered Priest Aldred as much as the Midwinter Fires; but I did not care. Hurriedly I knotted up the broken ends of the thong, and thrust the amber into the breast of my rough tunic. I smoored the fire, and pulled out somebody's spare cloak, for I had none of my own, and outside sleet was spitting down a chill north wind. I took Thormod's hunting-knife from the shelf above his sleeping-place, and thrust it into my belt. Then I opened the door that creaked on its sodden leather hinges, and ducked out into the night.

The King's forecourt was in almost as much of an uproar as the town below, and at Yule, no very careful watch was kept on the townward gate, or a thrall leaving the Garrison quarters after dark might have had to give account of himself. As it was, with the borrowed cloak hitched high to cover the thrall-ring round my neck, I got through easily enough, and plunged into the narrow winding ways where men surged to and fro with torches and jars of ale.

I made my way up one alley and down another, diving into ale-house after ale-house, peering into every shadowed or torchlit face I passed. Again and again I saw men from the Garrison, several times I came up with men of the *Sea Swallow*'s crew, but never a sign of Thormod. In a wine-shop down the boat-strand I even found Haki, but Thormod was not with him, having gone off on some business of his own.

By that time battles were beginning to break out in different parts of the town; and as I turned into the dark mouth of a wynd, heading back from the boat-strand towards St. Columba Church, a small vicious fight was spilling out from an open torchlit doorway at the far end. I saw a struggling knot of men, and caught the wicked dart of a knife blade; and in the same instant, out of the snarling worry of sound, a voice pitched to carry from end to end of a small war fleet against a full gale sent up the shout—'*Sea Swallow! Sea Swallow!* To me!'

I had heard that kind of shout before. It was the recognized signal by which any member of a ship's crew who ran into trouble could bring any and every shipmate within hearing racing to his aid. And I knew the voice. I'd have known it if it had come straight out of the Mouth of Hell.

I sent up the answering call—'*Sea Swallow* coming!'—and headed up the alleyway, freeing the hunting-knife from my belt as I ran, to hurl myself joyfully into the fight. In the midst of it, Thormod had got his back to a wall and was holding off, as best he could, some half-dozen Irishmen out for blood. I dived in, flinging one man off with my shoulder, ducked between two more, and came up at Thormod's side. Yelling faces were all about us. I felt Thormod's shoulder where mine pressed against it, and the smell of blood came up into the back of my nose. I saw the flash of a knife and brought up my own to meet it, and felt the jar as the two blades rang together. But for me the fight was almost as short as my fight with the cattle raiders. I turned aside another thrust, and I think got in a glancing stroke of my own; and then someone hooked my feet from under me, and I went down among the legs of the battle. Somebody's heel caught me on the old hurt on the side of my head. I was aware through a growing chaos of Thormod standing astride me, and above me in the reeling turmoil heard his voice lifted up in the great Viking war shout that I have heard since above half a score of battlefields, and then everything swam away into a buzzing mist. From somewhere a long way off, I was aware of a shout '*Sea Swallow* coming!' and a rush of feet up the wynd; and then after a time of swirling and trampling tumult, everything was suddenly quiet, and I was swimming up out of a darkness that was not just the darkness of the night. I was sitting up with my back against the wall. Torchlight was still spilling through the open doorway, and by its yellow glow somebody was heaving a jack of ice-cold water over my head. I gasped, and fumbled up a hand, and felt the stickiness of blood in the old place, and for a moment was not sure whether this was a new fight or still the time of the shore-killing.

'He's coming back,' somebody said.

And then Thormod's voice, with a kind of raw edge to it that I did not understand, came cutting through the confusion in my head. 'What in the Thunderer's name are you doing here?'

'Time enough for that later,' said Haki out of the night and the flurrying sleet. 'It's too wolf-dark for comfort down here, and no knowing how far we've driven them off.' He kicked something sprawling in the roadway, that groaned. 'I've no wish for a knife in my back, if you have.'

And another voice said, 'Up, you.'

I was already trying to scramble to my feet, but my legs seemed made of dough. Then Thormod's arm came round me, heaving me up. 'Here, Haki, take his other side, he's as wankle as a wet sark.'

'Poor shape for walking,' Haki agreed, and added, only half in jest, 'Well, if you think he's worth it. . . .'

'I do,' said Thormod. 'And remember, if I lose my thrall, you don't get your two gold pieces back.'

I never had any very clear idea of our journey back to quarters; but suddenly the warmth and shelter of the sleeping-bothy were about me, and Eric was kicking the smoored fire into a glow. I could stand alone, by that time, but the room still swam unpleasantly round me, and after a few moments, I collapsed by the hearth. Thormod dipped a pannikin into the ale crock in the corner and jolted it against my teeth, while Haki, who had a long shallow gash on one forearm, felt along the rafters for a wad of cobwebs to stop the bleeding.

My head was clearing, and I remembered the piece of amber, and began in sudden desperate haste to fumble in the breast of my tunic. It was still there. I pulled it out and held it to Thormod.

'Your piece of amber—the thong's broken and you must have pulled it off with your byrnie. I was afraid—I thought. . . .'

I was no longer quite sure what I had thought.

Thormod took it, quirking an eyebrow. It was as if he said, 'That harm might come to me without it?' though he did not speak the words. 'I'll put a fresh thong on it in the morning, but this will serve for now.' He slipped the thong over his head and stowed the great golden drop inside the neck of his sark.

I had got to the stage, that comes sometimes either with drink or a knock on the head, in which one has to make sure that everything is explained to the last detail. 'But I could not find you. Even Haki did not know where you were. And then I heard you shout—'

'Have another drink,' said Thormod. 'And so you came to my rescue.'

Eric snorted. 'Rescue! He must have gone charging in as blind as a bull-calf! He was on the ground with you standing across him, when we arrived!'

Thormod's sudden grin flashed across his face from ear to ear. 'That proves one thing, at least, that he was the first to reach me!'

By that time someone had kindled the resin torch in its sconce against the roof tree; and by its smoky light, those of the Brotherhood who had taken some scathe in the fight, were cleaning up the damage. Haki looked up from the gash on his forearm. 'Anyway, Thormod Sitricson, what were you doing, off on your own like that?'

'Hunting,' said Thormod.

'A girl? And somebody else's?'

'Oh no, a snow bear. I always hunt snow bears through the streets of Dublin after dark; they show up better that way.' Thormod threw the now empty pannikin at Haki's head, and laughter took them all, and went roaring through the crowded bothy.

Later, lying huddled in my usual night-time place across the doorway, I woke in the dark with the thrall-ring rubbing my neck, and moved to find an easier position, and drifted off to sleep again. But in the moment between waking and sleeping, it was not the thrall-ring that mattered to me most, but suddenly and warmly, the remembered feel of Thormod's shoulder against mine, mine against Thormod's, in the dark wynd.

5 A First Time for Everything

The year came slowly up out of the dark and turned again towards spring, the alders along the River Strand were flushed with rising sap, then green-misted with leaf buds bursting; and the crew of the *Sea Swallow* set to pitching her sides and overhauling her gear and rigging. And working with them, I still did not know what was going to be the next thing for me. I hoped desperately that Thormod meant to take me with him; I was almost sure, but never quite. He had never spoken of the matter, and I had never been able to get the question—such a small, simple question—past something that seemed to strangle it in my throat.

And then the day came when Sigurd, the Ship-Chief, went up to the King's Hall to claim the Farewell Gold, the final gift-pay that was due to them; and when he came back, they went down to the boat-shed as the custom was, for the share-out.

The *Sea Swallow*, almost ready for sea, lay out on the slipway in the early spring sunshine; but her mast, together with canvas and cordage and the like, was still stacked within the shed; and I have remembered always, when I think of that day, how the sunlight reflected off the water cast silvery ripple patterns into the darkness of the shed, over the faces of the men gathered there, wave-lighting, as though it were already at sea, the snarling fresh-painted dragon-head that would soon be shipped at the galley's prow.

Sigurd Ship-Chief counted out the money, Irish gold and coins from all the trading world, on the head of a water cask; and each

man came forward and took his share. And when the share-out
was over, and each man stowing his gold in his pouch, Thormod
took two coins from his own store, and tossed them over to Haki.
'Here. I pay my debt.'

Haki caught them, but did not at once add them to his own
pouch. 'It could have waited until you'd sold him.'

It seemed to me that there was a sudden silence. I heard the
water lapping against the slipway and the crying of the gulls, and
the sudden drubbing of my own heart.

Then Thormod said, 'I am not selling him.'

Eric said, 'What would you be needing with another thrall in
Svendale?'

'With another thrall, nothing. I am not minded to leave a man
who's fought shoulder to shoulder with me, sold off in a strange
land with a thrall-ring round his neck; that's all.'

He stowed his pouch away, and swung round, jerking his chin
at me as he did so. 'Come, then, we've business with Grim the
Smith.'

I heard the snort of surprised laughter behind us, as I followed
him out from the boat-shed, and up towards the smithy near the
gate of the King's forecourt, where Grim and his striker forged and
mended weapons for the men of the Garrison. He was beating out
the dint in a damaged shield boss, his boy behind him kneading
the goatskin bellows to keep the forge fire roaring.

He glanced up as Thormod checked in the doorway, and then
went on with his hammering. Thormod waited in silence, leaning
against the door-post. Nobody interrupts a smith at his art. After
a while, when the glow had darkened from the metal, Grim thrust
it back into the fire. Then he straightened up and looked at us
properly. 'What is it this time? Another sprung rivet?'

'A thrall-ring to be cut off,' Thormod said.

Grim's gaze slipped over his shoulder to myself standing behind
him. 'So? That makes a change. Bide while I finish this, it will not
take long.'

So we waited, hearing the ding-ding-ding of the light hand-
hammer, watching the sparks fly upward from the red dragon-
throat of the fire. I was being careful not to feel much; it was as
though once I started to feel, I might not be able to stop. But even
so, I had to clench my hands to stop them shaking.

At last Grim laid the finished work aside, and said, 'Now.'And took a mallet and a cold chisel from his tool bench, while the boy let the fire die down. 'Come you and kneel here.' I went forward and knelt where he bade me, beside the anvil. 'Your neck, so. Don't move unless you want to lose an ear.'

The stroke of the mallet on the chisel nearly jarred my head from my shoulders; but at the third blow the thing parted, and Grim laid down his tools and wrenched the iron ring open. I saw the blue knotted veins on his wrists and forearms stand out with the strain. I got up, rubbing my neck. Thormod gave him a coin, and we walked out of the smithy without a word spoken between us.

On the way up through the town, I had walked behind my master, but on the way down again, we walked side by side, shoulder brushing shoulder in the narrow ways, and still without a word, until we came out at the head of the Strand, above the boat-sheds and the bay. And then we checked and turned to look at each other.

'Well?' said Thormod, breaking the silence at last.

'Well?' I said.

'You're free.'

I asked slowly and carefully, 'What is it that I do with my freedom?'

'Whatever seems to you good. You've a head on you, and hands to your elbows. You could get yourself taken on by a shipmaster bound for Bristow. Or—'

Abruptly he reached out and laid a heavy arm across my shoulders. 'The *Sea Swallow* could do with another man for the rowing-benches.'

'I've never handled an oar,' I said slowly.

Thormod's long straight mouth quirked at the corners. 'You'll have learned the way of it before we come to Thrandisfjord, and have the blisters to prove it. . . . I may need a man to stand with me another day. Come, Jestyn.'

The grin that had flashed across his face had left it; and suddenly he was grave. We stood looking eye into eye; and for the first time it came to me that I need not have answered that shout in the dark alleyway at Yule; the Viking Kind meant nothing to me, and surely I owed him nothing because I was his thrall, bought whether

I would or no. I had answered because it was Thormod in need of help, and I was Jestyn. Thormod and Jestyn. Nothing to do with Dane and English, master and thrall. And Thormod knew it also. There has to be a first time for everything; for friendship as well as love; and first friendship, once given, can no more be given again than first love.

I was suddenly and piercingly aware of the wind off the bay and the sun-dazzle on the water, and the thin crying of the gulls wheeling with the evening light under their wings.

'I'll come,' I said.

I had my blisters, and the blisters broke and my hands were raw and then healed and beginning to harden, when, with the many days of our seafaring behind us, we rounded the North Ness into the cold blue-green waters of the Sound, and came down the east coast of Jutland, making for Thrandisfjord.

We made the fjord mouth towards evening; the shadows of the land lying out across the water, and the shore-birds crying. Inside the shoaling sandbanks, the water was quiet and deep, reflecting the alders and birches that grew down to the shore. The fjord swung northward, and as a fresh reach opened up, there was a little spur of land thrusting out into the water, and a man on it, lopping the branches from a fallen birch tree, who dropped his axe as we came in sight, and began to wave his arms and shout. The crew shouted back, cursing and joyful. And then the man turned and ran.

'Thord Loudmouth, first with the news as usual,' Haki said. And laughter swept the *Sea Swallow* from stem to stern; not because there was really so much to laugh at, but because her crew had been away so long and were home again. There was no familiar home waiting for me round the next bend of the fjord, but the heart-bursting, salt-stung, vomit-tasting days of the long seafaring were behind me, and I was a free man, and I followed Thormod. And so I was content enough.

Thord Loudmouth must have done his work well, for when we came to the landing beach, it seemed that all the folk of Thrandisfjord were there to meet us. We shipped oars and sprang overboard into the shallows, and ran the *Sea Swallow* up the gull-grey shingle; and men were greeting their women, and brother greeting brother, and a father tossing up a joyfully shrieking child, all along the brown sea-wrack of the waterline.

That night we all feasted in the Chief's Fire Hall. I mind how the fern-strewn floor still heaved gently under me with the long slow swell of the Northern Seas. And next morning the crew of the *Sea Swallow* split up, those whose homes were in the settlement biding where they were, the rest scattering to farms and steadings in other valleys.

Thormod and I and a few others set off southward. After an hour's walking over the moors, Haki went his separate way; and a while past noon we came to a cattle track that forded a stream and disappeared up a birch-wooded side valley, and Eric took it, while the rest of us pushed on up the stream bank. They had fought and slept and drunk together for more than a year, yet they parted as though they had been out on a day's hunting. Once, it would have seemed strange to me, but by now I had learned the ways of the Northmen.

By evening, Thormod and I were alone.

We took our shelter for the night in a little turf bothy on the moors between one valley and the next. A shieling where the herdsmen would live when the cattle were out on the summer pasture. We made a hunting fire of birchbark and heather snarls before the door-hole, and ate the ship's bannock and garlic-flavoured curds that we had brought with us; and washed it down with ice-cold water that I fetched in Thormod's war-cap from a little spring nearby. After we had eaten, we bided for a long while, feeding the fire with bits of birch bark, and talking or companionably silent as the mood took us—Thormod was always a good person to be silent with—alone in the sky-wide emptiness of the moors.

Thormod lay propped on one elbow, staring into the heart of the fire. Presently, maybe because he had been so long away and tomorrow's homecoming was so near, he began to talk of his own place and people, as he had never done before. Home and kinsfolk, father and brother and brother's wife, friends from other farms, who he had run with since he was a cub. Two friends in particular, Herulf and Anders Herulfson, from some steading further up the same valley. 'It was a near thing that Anders came with me to Ireland,' he said, 'a very near thing.'

'What happened, that he did not?' I asked; and wondered if I should have left the thing unsaid, for I could sense a hurt somewhere in him.

Thormod fed the fire with a sprig of dry heather, carefully waiting for the tip to flower into flame before he dropped it into the red heart. 'He had cast his eye on a girl. So he settled for a raiding summer—out after sheep shearing and back to get in the harvest. I'm thinking he'll be wed by now. Not that any woman would hold that one long to hearthfire and home acre. He was ever one for the wind in his sails.'

'Aren't you all, you of the Northmen Kind?' I said.

'Aye, I suppose so. The wandering is born in us. Though maybe if it were not for the leanness of our pastures . . . a poor land always casts its sons as a gorse-pod casts its seed in summer.' He laughed. 'Thor's Hammer! I sound like some greybeard that's been forty years West-over-seas! When Anders and Herulf and I stood not much higher than the hounds under the table, we forged plans to take the road to Miklagard and make our fortunes in the south. We'd been listening to merchants' stories.'

I nodded. I had not lived a winter among the Northmen of Dublin, and listened to their talk, without hearing of the golden fortress-city many months' journey to the south-east, where the Emperor of Byzantium sat on his golden throne; also of the long and perilous river-faring, followed mostly by the men of the Baltic shores, that was the road to Miklagard, and the strange and wonderful adventures to be had, and the fortunes to be made. . . . Merchants' stories, travellers' tales. . . . I suppose most boys listen to them, one time or another, and get a pang of the wander-hunger and dream a brightly-coloured dream or so. For myself, the wandering was in my feet also.

'This merchant had lumps of raw amber as big as my fist and as yellow as the sun,' Thormod was saying. 'Anders and Herulf traded him some more—just small bits; we used to go hunting it among the seawrack after a storm. He was taking it south to trade for wine and enamel work. He promised to tell us more stories when he came back, but we never saw him again.'

'You did not trade him your piece of amber.'

'Other pieces I did, but not this.' Thormod touched the breast of his byrnie. 'It seemed to me more beautiful than the reindeer-skin belt he would have given me for it. Also there was its shape. And the very day after I found it, I won the Boys' Wrestling Contest at the Thing Gathering, so I kept it for luck. I'm thinking you had maybe something of the sort in mind, the night you came after me with it through the darkest alleyways of Dublin.'

Abruptly, he rolled over and huddled himself in his cloak. 'I'm for sleep.'

I built up the fire against night-prowling creatures of the wild, thinking, as I laid the last thorn root over the red core, that it would be good if I were not following Thormod back into his own world, kinsfolk and old friends and old hounds, that would be none of mine, familiar fields where I should be a stranger. It would be good if we were setting out, the two of us, on some unknown road that led to the ends of the earth. Even the road to Miklagard, maybe.

And in that moment a little thin wind came sighing through the young heather; and I shivered, and the hair stirred on the back of my neck as though cold fingers had brushed it. I pushed the thought away. It was a bad thought, that took no heed of Thormod, but only of myself. An unchancy thought, and I wished that I could unthink it again.

I rearranged the thorn root with great care, pulled my cloak about me, and crawling back into the shelter of the bothy, lay down beside Thormod, with my feet to the fire.

6 Home-coming

Next morning we ate what remained of the bannock and set out on the last part of our journey. Over the moors, the curlews were in mating-call, and as the sun rose higher there began to be a warm scent of bog-myrtle in the air, mingling with the salt tang from the sea. Well on between noon and evening we came over a gentle ridge beyond which the land sank away to a broad shallow dale. And on the crest of the ridge, close beside the track, stood a tall lichened stone with what looked like a pair of eyes carved on it—carved long ago and half lost again to the wind and weather—and beside it, a wind-shaped thorn tree starred with sparse grey-white blossom. Thormod checked beside the stone, and touched it in a peculiar way. 'That is for home-coming,' he said. 'Next time we come this way, it will be for you to do that, also. . . . From here on, all this is Svendale. We're home, Jestyn.'

And we went on, following the herding track down into the sun-dappled cloud-shadowed dale.

Presently, with the shadows lengthening, I glimpsed brown-thatched roofs in the loop of an alder-fringed stream; and we were coming down between in-take fields laid up for hay and barley. I thought, so close in to the steading, to see folk at work, but everywhere seemed strangely empty of humankind. I looked questioningly aside at Thormod, and saw the frown line between his eyes as he glanced about him.

Something was wrong. No word passed between us, but Thormod lengthened his stride, and I did the same, following him, as we came down to the stream and splashed through the cattle ford.

Voices reached us at last, as we came up towards the steading gate; and the folk who had been missing from the fields were all there, gathered in the wide garth; and more beside, from farms up and down the dale, I guessed, old and young, men and women, children and hounds. Some of the hounds leapt up and raced, joyfully baying, to greet Thormod as we came in through the gate. But the folk, looking round to see who it was, glanced at one another and back again, and were oddly still; a kind of troubled and uncertain stillness. Something was wrong indeed, horribly wrong. And yet beyond the people, I could see trestles before the house-place door, spread as though for a feast. Someone cleared his throat as if to speak, and then was silent again. Then an old man with a long nose and a bright and expectant eye, the kind that likes to be the stirrer of trouble and the bearer of ill news, came out from the rest and pushed through the welcoming dogs.

'You are returned in a black hour, Thormod Sitricson.'

Thormod never looked at him. Whatever the trouble was, seemingly he did not want to hear it from that particular old man. He thrust the dogs aside and walked on towards the house-place. The dogs, suddenly fallen from their high spirits, followed him. So, with some idea of keeping close to him in case of need, did I.

Before the house-place, the women were bending over the long trestle boards, setting out platters of meat and bannocks and great jugs of ale. They also checked into that odd stillness at the sight of Thormod; and one of them, who seemed, young though she was, to be the mistress of the house, turned and called through the doorway into the darkness beyond it, 'Sitric, it is Thormod come home.'

In answer, someone loomed into the doorway; a man somewhat like Thormod but a few years older, taller and darker, and of a blunter make. 'Thormod, my brother! You have heard?'

They put their arms round each other's shoulders, and pulled close a moment. 'No. I am straight come from Thrandisfjord,' Thormod said. And then, 'Is it our father?'

'It is our father.'

They went in together, and I—I followed still, much as a hound might have done.

They went down the long central aisle between the stalls where the cattle would be housed in winter. There was torchlight at the far end where it widened out into the family's living space. No firelight, for the fire had been quenched on the hearth; and the torches burned at the head and feet of a dead man, who lay under a great brown bearskin in the midst of the place. The fur was pulled up to his throat; and Sitric stooped without a word, and drew it back a little way.

I had checked between the last of the cow-stalls, and saw nothing of what was beneath. But I saw Thormod's back grow rigid, and his hands clench at his sides into quivering fists.

'Who killed him?'

Sitric let the rug fall back. 'Anders and Herulf Herulfson—either or both.'

'Anders? Herulf? That's madman's talk!' Thormod began shouting; then he checked and quietened. 'What was the way of it?'

Sitric told him, in a dead level voice, standing over their father's body. 'We have had trouble with the wolfkind, this spring. Five days since, our father went hunting. He'd a new bow to try out, and you know what he was like with something new. He hunted late, and at dusk he saw what he thought was a wolf among the alder woods up the back. It was too dark to see properly, but he let fly. . . .'

'And it was not a wolf,' Thormod said.

'It was Herulf Blackbeard in his old wolfskin cloak.'

'And so Anders and Herulf took up the Blood Feud.'

'The Thing was summoned to try the case. I suppose as it was an ill-chance killing, the Lawman would have ordered that we pay the man-price, and that would have been the end of it. But Herulf and Anders. . . . They must have got him while he was out riding the lower sheep-run. Yesterday at first light they came across by Loud Beck and flung his body down by the Mark Stone, and shouted to Ulf, who was taking out the cattle, that they were not waiting for the Greybeards of the Thing Council, and that they set more store by blood than Wyr Geld, in payment for their father's death. Then they rode off southward.'

'What possessed Father to ride out alone along the lower run?' Thormod said after a moment.

'Maybe he thought they would wait for the Thing, and abide by its ruling.'

'And maybe he knew that they would not; and thought that he'd had the best part of his life, and thought that his death, alone, would come cheaper than his death along with the rest of you, and the farm burned over your heads in the good old-fashioned way.' Thormod did not speak accusingly, as though to say 'Why did you let him go alone?' but only as one stating facts. I come of a people who do not howl and cast ashes on their heads for the death of kinsfolk; but this was something that I had not met before.

And then in the same level, fact-stating tone, he added, 'Herulf-stead shall burn for this.'

'In the good old-fashioned way? You'll not find the young wolves in the lair.'

'Where, then?'

I thought for a moment that Sitric was looking at me. Then I saw that his gaze had gone over my shoulder to someone coming up behind me; and a big man with a thrall-ring on his neck slouched past me into the torchlight. Thormod turned and saw him.

'Ulf?'

The thrall swallowed harshly. 'They shouted—Anders shouted to me before they rode off—to tell anyone who asked, that the amber merchant must have some more good stories by now, and they were away to find him.'

Sitric looked at his brother. 'Does that have any meaning for you?'

Thormod nodded. 'Aye. Because it was meant for me.'

'So? What meaning, then?'

'That Anders and Herulf knew that I also would not settle for the Wyr Geld. They have set out for Miklagard.'

'It's not like those two to run,' Sitric said.

'Who spoke of running? No man sits twiddling his thumbs waiting for death under his own blazing thatch, if he can play the game another way. And they also had kin to think of. But they leave me word where to meet them.'

'They leave *us* word,' Sitric said, troubled but staunch.

'Na, the message was for me. You are the eldest, and you have a wife; it is for you to bide here and hold the steading together. Our grandfather did not in-take it from the wild, that we should both take the road to Miklagard and leave it to go back to the wild again.'

Sitric Sitricson was silent a moment, looking down at the stark face above the bearskin rug, as though he were uncertain. He would always be a little uncertain, I thought, one who needed time to make up his mind. 'Aye well, we can quarrel as to that later,' he said at last. 'They are gathered to the Arval in the garth, and we should go out to them.'

They turned towards the entrance aisle. Ulf was already gone, and I slipped out ahead of them quickly into the fading daylight, where the pine-knot torches had just been lit and were making a black resin-scented smoke that curled away sideways on the light wind, and folk were already crowding to the food and drink, while a blind harper who had wandered in from somewhere with his dog beside him, sat on the end of a bench, tuning his harp.

Somewhere near at hand a cow was lowing, for it was past milking-time. And feeling myself a stranger among all these folk who were Thormod's folk and none of mine, I turned in search of the cattle fold that was something familiar in an alien world.

I was leaning over the hurdle gate, snuffing the warm comforting smell of the beasts, when I heard Thormod's great shout raised above the voices and the harpsong behind me. '*Sea Swallow! Sea Swallow!* To me!' And knew the call was for me.

So I left the friendly cattle and went back into Thormod's world, into the crowd and the flare of torches before the house-place door.

And then Thormod's arm was across my shoulders, and Thormod was swinging me round to the torchlit faces, saying, 'Here he is—Jestyn, my shoulder-to-shoulder-man—come back with me from West-over-seas!'

7 The Blood Brotherhood

Afterwards, through the fog of next morning's headache, I had very little memory of that funeral feast. Only one thing I remembered clearly: and that, when the night was already worn on a good way, was Thorn, the blind harper, getting to his feet, saying, 'Now I will make a new song—a song for the two who go out from here with the mark of the Blood Feud on their foreheads. Two brothers against two brothers, who will not turn back before all be finished, and the Death songs sung for those who are to die.' And I was vaguely wretched, and took no heed of the song at all.

That day, the Master of Sitricstead was home-laid among his kin, and the folk from other farms all went away. And in the dark of the following night I woke in the loft above the cattle stalls, and found Thormod missing from his hollow in the hay beside me.

At first I thought that he had gone out to make water, and would soon be back; and I lay watching a white line of moonlight that slipped through a chink in the thatch, and waiting. But the white line moved to pick out a bent grass-stem, to a dry cloverhead, casting its tiny clear shadow below it; and he did not come. And then fear came upon me. I had taken it as a settled thing that I was going with Thormod on the road to Miklagard, but as it had been when the *Sea Swallow* was made ready for the homeward way, so it was now. No word actually spoken between us. And Dark Thorn had sung of two brothers. . . . But that did not really fit, because it had been settled that Sitric was to bide with the steading. . . . I was too much afraid to think straight, or I might have taken comfort from that.

How if Thormod had sought to avoid all farewells by slipping away in the night and leaving us simply to wake in the morning and find him gone on his lonely road? If I had stopped to look about me, I would have seen that his few belongings were still where he had left them. But fear had me by the throat.

I had lain down to sleep in the usual way in breeks and under-sark, and had only to pull on my raw-hide shoes and rough wadmal tunic, and stick in my belt the hunting-knife that was my only possession, and I stood ready to go.

Then, torn between the need for speed and the need for silence, I slid over the edge of the loft floor, felt with my feet for the edge of the cattle stall beneath, and dropped as lightly as I could into the central aisle.

In the living-place at the far end, I could just make out the red glow of the smoored fire. One of the dogs stirred and growled a little, though not much for they were used to night-time comings and goings, and Sitric cursed him without properly waking up, from the big box bed. I checked, holding my breath, and the dog subsided, grumbling; and I went on. The door was on the snib, as Thormod must have left it, and I opened it as silently as might be, and slipped out and across the sleeping steading-garth. The hurdle gate had been hauled aside. Thormod had certainly gone that way, but would he have left it open if he were not coming back? Doubt began to creep in beside the fear within me, but I had to know. I had to know.

So I too stepped out on to the track, my moon-shadow running beside me. There was no one on the track so far as the ford or on the rising slope beyond it. But just across from the steading gate was the apple garth, the trees just breaking into blossom, small and wind-shaped, bent all one way. The kind whose apples are scarcely worth eating at harvest but withered and yellow and honey-sweet at Midwinter. The moon filled the place with dapplings and stripes of black and silver, and markings of a wildcat's hide. Almost anything could have been among those trees, so long as it did not move. Then something, someone, did move, on the path that skirted the trees on its way down from the fellside. A moment more, and I saw that it was Thormod. He checked and looked back the way he had come, up towards the dark hummock on the open fell, where we had home-laid the old Master of Sitricstead that morning. Then I knew that he had indeed been about his farewells; taking leave of his father, now, rather than in the day-light before the eyes of other men. Taking whatever vows he had to take, apart from the customary vows of vengeance that he had taken, half drunk, and bragging of its bloody splendour, at the Arval the night before. There are things that a man needs to do by himself, and I knew then that I should not have come. I was turning back, but my foot caught a loose stone in the side of the track and sent it rolling; and Thormod swung round.

'Who? Jestyn, you again!'

'I—it was a mistake—' I stammered. 'I'll away back—'

'No, but why did you come?' Thormod came out on the track, and touched his breast, where the piece of amber hung beneath his sark. 'I did not leave it behind me this time. Did you think I needed your shoulder against mine in this also?'

'I was afraid you had gone without me.' I sounded like a child in my own ears.

'Do you think I would do that, not even telling you?' he said, seriously.

'I—no—but I woke and you were gone. Maybe I'm still stupid with ale—I've never had so much before. But—*I come with you!*'

There was a moment's pause, and I heard the faint stirring of wind through the apple boughs. Then Thormod said, 'Do you? I take up the Blood Feud for my father's death, but there is no call for you to follow the same road.'

'Your road is mine also. Two against two makes a fair fight.'

' "Two brothers against two brothers." So said Blind Thorn.'

'I had all but forgotten that,' I said.

'Never forget what Thorn says. The eyes of his body do not see as other men see, but he has another kind of seeing.' Thormod held out his hand. 'You have your knife on you? Give it to me.'

I pulled the knife from my belt, and he took it and turned his left hand palm upward. In the white fire of the moonlight I saw the paler skin inside his wrist, and the place where the blue veins branched as the veins of an iris petal. He drew the point of the knife across, leaving a line like a dark thread in its wake. A few beads of blood sprang out, black in the moonlight; and he gave me the knife. 'Now you.'

I made the same cut across my own wrist, and we rubbed the mouths of the two cuts together. A few drops spattered down and were lost in the long grass, and the thing was done.

'Now we are one blood, you and I,' Thormod said. 'Two brothers against two brothers. Now the sign of the Blood Feud is on your forehead also, as Dark Thorn saw it, and my road is your road, to Miklagard and beyond.'

So I took up the Death Feud, the Blood Feud for a man I had never seen living.

And we went back to the warm darkness of the hayloft for the rest of the night. And next morning Thormod took leave of his kin, and we set out. We rode a couple of scrub ponies; and for the first time in my life I felt the slap of a sword against my thigh, the pull of the sword-strap over my shoulder. It was an old sword from the weapon kist, the wolfskin sheath worn almost bare in places, the wooden grip darkened by other men's sweat, but the blade oiled and keen. I wondered how long it would be before the grip felt familiar in my hand, and the blade answered to my will.

So we took the road to Miklagard.

Some days later, we sold the ponies at Aarhus, where the Great Sound opens south into the Baltic Sea. And that same evening, while we sat in a waterside ale-shop under an old ship's awning, with a pot of ale and a platter of pig-meat between us, a man turned in from the alleyway outside, spoke to the old one-legged pirate who kept the place, then came threading his way through the elbows and sprawling feet to the corner where we sat. He was rangy and loose-limbed, so tall that his rough sandy hair brushed the salt-stained canvas overhead, with a fair, freckled skin, and grey-green sea-water eyes.

'Which of you is Thormod Sitricson?' he asked.

'I am,' Thormod said.

'So. You have been asking in the town, for two men.'

'Aye.'

'Would there be a drink in it, for me?'

'If you can tell me where they are, and if they are the right men, as much drink as you can hold without bursting like an old wine-skin.'

The man hitched up a stool and sat down, leaning his elbows on the ale-stained trestle boards. 'Anders and Herulf Herulfson, are their names; and one of them—Anders, it would be?—has a small scar on his cheek-bone, and odd eyes, one blue, one grey.'

Thormod nodded. 'Where are they?'

'I am thirsty,' said the man, and grinned.

Thormod looked at him a moment, then turned and shouted to the potboy, 'Drink, here!'

A brimming ale jug was brought, and the man hitched it towards him. 'Drink heil!' he said, and poured about half the jugful down his throat.

'Wass heil!' Thormod drank also. 'Where are they?'

The man set down the jug and wiped the back of his hand across his mouth. 'Not here.'

'I did not think they would be.' Thormod reached out and re-moved the jug. They were grinning at each other, enjoying every moment of the game. 'And I'd no mind to waste my time hunting them through Aarhus, and them already away. When did they sail? And what ship?'

'Three days ago.' The man took back the jug, drank again, and set it down. 'They came to us of the *Red Witch* first. Hakon Ketilson is gathering a crew for the Kiev voyage and on to Mikla-gard; but the *Serpent* was sailing a few days ahead of us; and they seemed eager to be away.'

'They would be,' Thormod said.

The other cocked an eyebrow. 'Friends of yours?'

There was a small sharp silence. Then Thormod said, 'Until my father killed theirs by mischance; and they cried Blood Feud, and killed mine.'

'So-o! *That* is the way of it! Small wonder they took oar with the *Serpent* rather than wait for the *Red Witch*. Yet they took no pains to cover their tracks.'

'They would not be hiding their tracks,' said Thormod into the ale-pot, and passed it to me.

The other stared at him a moment, then shrugged and turned again to his own drink. And in a little, Thormod said, 'Would this Hakon Ketilson of yours be still gathering his crew?'

'If it was me,' said the man, 'I'd appeal to the Judgement of the Thing, and accept their settlement as to Wyr Geld. Blood will not bring the old wolf back, and gold has always its uses.'

Watching Thormod, I saw his eyes slowly widen, fixed on the other's face, and the muscles stiffen in his neck. 'Yet for the old wolf—blood may give him the better right to sit with his head high in Valhalla.'

I was a Christian of sorts. I had thought of the Blood Feud as a matter of vengeance. It was not until that moment that I understood that for Thormod and his kind, it was a matter of a dead man's honour. I was learning fast.

'Each to his own way,' the man said. 'Yours, then, is to Kiev?'

'And beyond to Miklagard if need be. Shall we go now and speak with this Ship-Chief of yours, while maybe he still has need of two more rowers?

'The lad comes with you, then?' The man jerked his chin in my direction.

'Jestyn, my blood-brother, comes with me. Aye.'

'So, now we are getting to names. Thormod and Jestyn—and I am called Orm. Now we are name-friends, almost shipmates. Another jug of ale, and we'll drink to a fortunate river-faring, and a fine bloody end to your feuding, before we go.'

So another jug of ale was brought, and we drank, passing it among the three of us. 'Wass heil! Drink heil! Wass heil!'

8 The River and the Trees

In the dusk of the short summer night, we ran Hakon Ketilson to earth in the ale-house where he was drinking with others of the *Red Witch*'s crew.

A square, squat man, with a face that looked as though it had been hewn from old ships' timbers, and only one eye, but that a very bright one that looked as though it did not miss much. He looked us over with it, and clearly he was one to pick his crews and not take any boat-strand garbage that drifted his way. But Orm claimed us for friends of his, forgetting to mention the fact that our friendship was barely an hour old. And so, in a little, we each took the knucklebone which Hakon produced out of a greasy pouch, and found ourselves part of the *Red Witch*'s crew; and together with the rest, we drank to good fortune and fair winds; and at last wavered our way down the boat-strand, with arms about each other's shoulders, singing, to spend what was left of the night huddled under the *Red Witch*'s awning, where she lay ready for the launch.

Two days later, with the stores and trade goods safely stowed in the narrow space beneath the deck planking, we ran her down into the water, and swung out the oars for Bornholm and the Baltic.

But weather-luck was not with us. We ran into a northerly gale and spent five days storm-bound in the lea of Bornholm's Western tip; and when we came at last into the broad mouth of the Dvina, with its trading post of wattle and tarred canvas sprawling among the river marshes, and stopped to water ship and take on last-minute stores, the *Serpent* was eleven days ahead of us.

'Small matter,' said Thormod. 'It is a long road to Miklagard.'

I remember two things chiefly of those first weeks of our river-faring: one is the unceasing, back-breaking hard work, and the other is the forest—the black, whispering pine forest that crowded to the banks on either side, as though it would have engulfed and smothered the river and the *Red Witch* and us toiling rowers along with it.

Sometimes the Dvina was wide enough for four vessels to pass abreast; and from time to time we met other ships making the return trip with embroidered linens and slave-girls and great jars of southern wine. When the river was broad so that the current slackened, if there was a following wind we would hoist the square sail and get a bit of help from that. But for the most part, it was just rowing, pulling up-river all day long against the current; day after day swinging to and fro to the oars, and the forest crawling by, black and unchanging so that it might have been the same stretch of trees every day.

At night we landed, and pulled the *Red Witch* up the bank, and made camp. Most times we fished for our supper, fresh fish being better than dried meat that grew more maggoty every day. Once or twice, when we made camp early enough, some of us would go off hunting, but without much success, scarce anything moves in those forests except the great bearded wild oxen—not the kind of beast to be easily knocked over in a spare hour after the day's work.

And at night, too, beside the camp-fire, Thormod would get up and draw his sword—one did not go unarmed in that country, no matter how much the day's work might be over and the time come for rest—and stand watching me until I got up and drew likewise. Then, however tired we were, we would fall to, cut and thrust and parry; the great sweeping strokes of the blades catching the light of fire and pine-knot torches. For it was on that long river-faring that he taught me, who had been a cowherd and a thrall, to be something of a fighting man.

Aye, there was hard work enough, those long river weeks, even without the sword-training at the day's end; and some of us muttered darkly as time went by, grumbling that Hakon Ship-Chief demanded too long at the oars each day. But there was a harder stretch to come.

'When you come to the Great Portage, you'll learn what work is,' Hakon said to those of us who hadn't made the trip before. And when we came to the Great Portage, we learned indeed.

The Dvina that flows north to the Baltic, and the Dnieper that goes looping southward past Kiev to the Inland Sea, rise many days apart in the dark forest heart of things; and ships making the river-faring must be man-handled across country from one to the other.

Where the portage-way started out from Dvina, there was a small settlement of the Rus; Northmen who had settled down with women of the forest tribes; narrow-eyed, high-cheeked tribesmen, and others of mixed stock between the two, who made their living from the ship folk passing by. From them, Hakon hired ten oxen with their drivers, and a kind of sledge to carry the goods and gear (for one lightens ship of all things movable, for a portage); and great runners for lashing along the *Red Witch*'s keel. We laid in a store of pitch and pork-fat for greasing the hauling gear; and on a grey day with mosquitoes hanging in stinging clouds under the trees, we started out.

'There are men who make this portage every year or so,' said Orm. 'It must be that someone dropped them on their heads when they were very small.'

With eight of the oxen harnessed to the *Red Witch*, and the remaining two to the sledge, it might have seemed that the crew would have an easy time of it. But we had constantly to scout ahead, making sure that the portage-way, cut deep through the forest, was clear of branches and fallen trees; and we toiled at the great rollers, pulling each one from beneath the ship's stern as it came free, and racing forward to set it beneath her forward-lurching prow. We must keep the runners daubed with pig-fat whenever they started to smoke. And though the oxen could keep her moving on the level, whenever the way ran up-hill, it needed all our strength and straining added to theirs to keep her going; while on a downhill stretch, we must dig in our heels and hang on to the check-ropes, lest she run wild and kill the oxen and maybe wreck herself into the bargain. And I was not the only one to have the feeling that the *Red Witch*, unhappy on land, was fighting us every step of the way.

So we toiled and sweated and cursed our way across country,

filling the forest with the noise of our going. The forest that gave back no sound out of its own darkness, save the hush of a little wind among the fir tops, that never reached us, sweating down below; and now and then the harsh alarm cry of some bird. But on the evening of the eighth day, we came over a last ridge, and saw before us through the trees, the dark shining loop of a river, and the same kind of rough settlement as the one at the Dvina end of the portage.

Someone let out a hoarse shout. 'The Dnieper!'

But Hakon Ship-Chief laughed. 'Not yet, though it runs into the Dneiper. The tribesmen have some name for it that no one else can get their tongues round. Mostly, our folk call it Beaver River.'

'But it *is* the end of the portage?' said Thormod, just ahead of me, somewhat breathless, for we were hanging on to one of the check-ropes.

'Aye, it's the end of the portage. Clear water now, down to Kiev.'

We feasted that night in company with the crew of a northward bound trader who were for the portage-way the next morning; sharing food and cooking fires and the news of North and South. Presently Thormod asked for news of the *Serpent*. 'You'll have passed her a few days since?'

'Aye.' The stranger Ship-Chief counted on his fingers. 'We shared camp one night. She'll be ten or twelve days ahead of you. But she'll not make it through to Miklagard this season.'

'Why would that be?' demanded Hakon Ship-Chief. 'There'll be open water out of Kiev for more than two moons yet.'

The other man spat a gobbet of pig gristle into the fire. 'It's not the ice that'll hold her, but Prince Vladimir. He'll be having a use for extra ships and fighting crews.'

We all pricked up our ears, and Hakon said, 'What use? Having said so much, say more, friend.'

I mind sitting with my arms across my knees, and my eyes full of firelight, half asleep after the day's labour, and listening to the 'more' that the man had to say. After more than a year among the Northmen, I knew something of the background to it. I knew that Byzantium had been at war for a good while with a people called the Bulgars, whose frontiers ran with their own. I knew that not so long since, the Bulgars had swarmed south into a part of the Empire called Greece, and that the Emperor Basil II had led an army into the heart of Bulgaria in return, and got very much the worst of it there. Also I seemed to have heard that while he was out of the way, two of his generals—both had given trouble before, and one been exiled and one given the post of Commander of Asia, which came to much the same thing—had seized their chances, and each gathered all the troops he could lay hands on and proclaimed himself Emperor; which made four, because Basil had a younger brother, Constantine, who officially shared the throne with him, though he cared more about dancing-girls and feasting than he did about ruling an Empire.

It had all sounded very complicated and somehow rather comic, when I had heard men talking of it in ale-houses in Dublin or round a driftwood fire in Aarhus, discussing its effects on trade with southern markets. But somehow, though just as complicated, it didn't seem so comic now.

'Just the day before we were due to sail,' the stranger Ship-Chief was saying, 'a Byzantine Red-ship came up-river, with three men on her afterdeck—two of them high-ranking officials of some sort, I'd say. And one a soldier; you could glimpse the mail under his silks. . . . Well, you know how it is; by next morning word of their business with Vladimir was all over Kiev. One of the generals who revolted—Bardas Phocas—'

'That's the Commander of Asia?' put in Hakon.

'Aye; that's the one—has got the upper hand of the other—Bardas Schlerus—and penned him up in one of his own fortresses—'

'If I make the Miklagard run yearly till I'm a hundred, I shall never find my way among these outland names!'

'And most of Schlerus' troops have rallied under Phocas's banner, to march on Miklagard. They're at Chrysopolis now; nose to nose with the city, as you might say, across just that narrow strip of water that they call the Bosphorus. And what's left of Basil's troops are mostly still away in the west, holding back the Bulgars So the Emperor Basil is sweating.'

'It is in my mind that well might the Emperor Basil be sweating,' said Hakon, throwing a bone over his shoulder to the hungry dogs that scavenged about the fire. 'And so he sends envoys to Prince Vladimir? Maybe there is a new Viking wind a-blowing.'

'Aye, the same thought was in all our minds; and the thought that with such a wind blowing, Vladimir was not one to sit at home with his sail furled. If he agreed to help the Emperor, he'd be wanting ships—all the ships he could lay his hands on here and now, beside sending north for more. So we finished loading in a hurry, and I, the Ship-Chief, went up to the Palace and told him we were pulling out for home, and offered to carry his ship summons for him. That way, we got clear ourselves.'

In the silence, somebody leaned forward and put a fresh branch on the fire. Smoke was the only thing to keep off the stinging clouds of mosquitoes that made life a torment after sundown.

'Some nerve, that must have taken,' Orm whistled softly. 'I doubt this Lord Vladimir is one who likes his thoughts being put to him, before he has had time to think them himself!'

'Some nerve, yes. But behold, we are free and on our homeward way.'

Thormod was looking intently at Hakon; I was watching Thormod; and above us the fir tops whispered together in the little wind that never reached the ground.

Then Hakon said, 'All this, you told to the *Serpent*'s crew, and still they held on for Kiev? How was it different, between them and you?'

The other grinned. 'They were heading south anyway. And did you know any of the Northern Kind to turn back from a fight when there was a fight brewing? All other things being equal. For us it *was* different; we'd made our trading trip, and a good one, too. We were heading north, and we'd been long away from home.'

'We also are heading south anyway, and are not yet hungry for our homes. And it is in my mind that a man grows rusty like a sword-blade, if he holds too long to the ways of peace.' Hakon's one little bright eye was suddenly dancing in his battered face. 'How say you, brothers?'

The crew of the *Red Witch* gave tongue in agreement, to a man.

Thormod and I looked at each other, and let our breaths go, gently.

9 Six Thousand Fighting Men

Next morning Hakon paid off the ox drivers, and we ran the *Red Witch* down into the water and set off on our river-faring once again. The worst was behind us now. The flow of the river was with us instead of against; and sometimes we could just let it take us, with the steersman at the stern and a few men rowing.

We passed high-piled beaver dams that choked the water here and there into dark spreading lagoons; and presently villages began to appear on the banks, and the fir trees that had hemmed us in so long began to give place to open woodlands of ash and elm and a kind of sycamore already touched with the first fires of autumn. Soon there were stretches of grassland too. It was so good to be able to see wide skies again, and let the eyes go free into a distance. And all the while, day by day, the river broadened, until at last we came into the great Dnieper.

And on an evening of clear long lights, and a fresh north wind ruffling the water, and with our dragon-head at the prow, and every man on the oars, we brought the *Red Witch* swinging down the last stretch of the river, round a last bluff of the western shore, and saw, over our shoulders, the crowding roofs of a town rising from the boat-sheds and crowded jetties along the waterfront, to the high halls along the hillcrest that caught the westering light as though they were brushed with gold. The evening smoke of cooking-fires making a blue haze over all, and the shadows lying long across the water and Kiev marches.

Kiev, the High City of the Rus, that had become so when the

Northmen first pushed south from their earliest settlements round Novgorod. Kiev, spreading its power up and down the great rivers and through the forests and across the empty steppe-lands, where-ever the Viking breed had made their land-take, wherever they had bred their own blue eyes and fair hair into the darkness of the Tribes; wherever they held the trade and the weapons. But I knew little of that at the time, and my foremost thought, as we came down the last stretch towards the crowded wharves, and the shadow of the city fell across us, was that somewhere among the long dark shapes of the shipping must be the *Serpent*; and on board, or somewhere among the crowded ways of the town, Anders and Herulf, waiting for our coming.

And a shadow that was more than the shadow of the city seemed to fall across me. I snatched a glance at Thormod swinging to and fro to the oar beside me; but his face, what I could see of it, was shut, and told me nothing.

'Lift her! Lift her!' came the chant of Hakon, Ship-Chief at the steering oar.

We brought the *Red Witch* in to the boat-strand and ran her up the beach clear of the river-line; and when we had made all secure, Hakon took about half of us, and leaving the rest on guard, set off for the hall of one of Prince Vladimir's nobles, who it seemed was a friend of his from past river-farings.

We left the shipyards and the merchants' quarter beside the Dnieper, and turned to the steep streets that led up towards the Prince's palace. We soon learned to call it the Khan's palace, for Vladimir, we found, had lately taken to himself the title of Khan, which until then had belonged to the Tribes. I suppose that was to show that he was the Lord of the Tribes as well as of the North-men. But that day it was still, to us, the Prince's palace.

The steep narrow streets were paved with logs, and wound in and out between log-built, turf-roofed houses, that were set back, each behind its own byres and fenced cattle-yard. Erland Silkbeard had his hall nearly at the top of the hill, only a little below the encircling turf walls of the palace itself. It was much like any other timber hall of the Northmen; like the Chief's Hall at Thrandisfjord, I thought, glancing about me as we came to the gate; but the byres and store-sheds and sleeping lodges gathered about the big central hall were many of them joined to each other and to the far end of the hall itself, so that one would be able to pass the length and breadth of the place without going out of doors. 'They have grown soft, these Northmen of the south,' I thought, not yet having known the cold of a winter night at the heart of the Rus Lands.

But there was not much time, just then, for looking round, for the Master of the Hall was just returned from hawking. He had that moment dismounted, his big goshawk still on his fist, and his horse was being led stableward as we came into the forecourt; a tall, long-boned man with a beard the colour of ripe barley, who wore his soft leather boots and goatskin jerkin as though they were dark silks. When he saw us, he gave the hawk to one of his hearth companions, and came striding across the forecourt. Hakon stumped forward to meet him with a shout, and they came together mid-way, flinging their arms round each other like a couple of bearcubs at play.

'Erland Silkbeard!'

Erland held our Ship-Chief at arm's length, and looked at him out of long dark eyes that were not like a Northman's at all. 'Hakon Ketilson! Hakon One-Eye! So the amber wind blows you south again!'

'Aye, and I am come in the old way, to claim Guest-right at your hearth, for me and my men.'

'And warm is your welcome!' Erland said. 'And long shall you bide at my hearth, this time of coming!'

'As long as may be, so that we are clear before ice closes the way south.'

'Longer than that, my friend.'

Hakon cocked his head on one side. 'Ah-huh! the tale was true, then? We shared camp fires with a north-bound crew at this end of the Great Portage, and heard a tale of an embassy from Miklagard, seeking help against troubles within the Empire. They had got their ship out quickly, lest, if the Lord Vladimir was minded to honour the old treaty, he should cast his eye on her to swell his war-fleet.'

'That will be the crew that carry his Ship Summons north with them,' said Silkbeard. 'He was a bold man, that Ship-Chief. . . . Aye, the tale was true. And so you come to join the fight?'

'Did ever you know Hakon One-eye or the men who sailed with

him to turn back from sword-clash? Besides, we were not minded to carry our cargo home again.'

'So; you will have long enough to see to your merchanting, and the *Red Witch* shall pass her winter safe and welcome in one of my own boat-sheds.'

'There is a moon and more before the ice,' Hakon said. 'What do we wait for?'

'Vladimir has promised two hundred ships, six thousand fighting men. Such a war fleet cannot be gathered and away before the ice closes the Dnieper, therefore it must wait until the ice breaks in the spring.' Erland, his hand still on Hakon's shoulder, turned back towards his hall. 'Come your ways in—already there's nip in the air once the sun is down. I will send men to see to the *Red Witch*, and bring up the rest of your crew.'

The next night, when the evening meal was over in Erland's hall, and Erland's men and *Red Witch* men together, we were sprawling at our ease with loosened belts while the great jars of ale and fermented mares' milk went round, Hakon leaned forward with his elbows on the table, and asked, 'What is it that they are building up yonder beside the Khan's palace?'

'There are always new buildings going up in Kiev, even beside the Khan's palace,' Erland said, making gentle finger-play with his beard, in the way he had. 'We are a growing city.'

'But this was a strange shape.' Hakon dipped his finger in his ale cup, and drew something on the table boards. 'Somewhat the shape of a God-House of the White Kristni.'

Erland nodded, and I had a feeling he was amused, not at Hakon but at the thing they were talking about. 'Aye, so.'

'And a man was overseeing the work. A dark fellow, with his hair cut—so.' Hakon drew the finger round his head, outlining a priest's tonsure. 'And garments on him such as the priests of the White Kristni wear, in Miklagard.'

Erland was leaning back against the red and saffron hangings on the wall behind him. He was a man who could relax more than most men, like a cat lying out in the sun. (But he could spring like a cat, too.) 'There are three such men in Kiev. They are here to teach us how to build this new kind of God-House beside the Khan's palace, and how to worship the White Kristni in it when it is built.' He looked round at our startled faces in the flare of the resin torches, and laughed. 'Nay now, it is simple enough. Our great Khan Vladimir has thought in his mind, that for a great people such as we have grown to be, the gods that we brought with us from our old world in the north are too rough-hewn, too homespun. We must take to the gods of the world that we now reach out to. We must turn to Islam or to the faith of the White Kristni.' He held out his silver-bound drink-horn to one of the women for refilling, and took a long drink before he went on. 'Islam, he finds, will not serve, for the followers of the Prophet Muhammad may drink no fermented liquor, and a faith which forbids a man his drink is clearly no faith for the Northmen.'

Hakon nodded, seeing the point. 'And so it must be the White Kristni.'

'In the spring, we sent men to Miklagard, to ask more concerning this faith. They came back in early summer, with what they had learned. And with strange stories beside—' The faint sheen of amusement that was so much a part of him faded for the moment, and he seemed grave, almost puzzled. 'They said that they were taken to a great gathering in the chief God-House of the city— St. Sophia, the Church of the Holy Wisdom. And there was wonderful singing and strange-smelling magic smoke that made their heads swim; and at the moment of the Sacrifice—they have a make-believe Sacrifice, pretending like children that bread and wine are the body and blood of their God—at the moment of Sacrifice, strange-winged spirits came down from the high roof, and hovered above their heads; and by this, they judged that the faith was a true and a powerful one.'

Since then, I have worshipped many times in the Church of the Holy Wisdom. I have heard the singing soar and swell and echo under the vast domes, till it is like no singing of this world; and seen how, in the light of the candles and the swirling incense smoke, the wonderful jewel-bright angels of the roof mosaics can seem to float free and swim down. . . . Now, I have a fairly clear idea as to the marvels that convinced Khan Vladimir's envoys. . . . Ah well, the Mysteries are in men's souls and hearts, that can receive the Truths of another world through the Truths of this one. . . .

At the time, I could only listen and marvel with the rest.

'Wah!' said Orm, speaking for the first time. 'That is a wonder indeed! Yet it is hard for a man to forsake the gods he has known all his life, for a strange God who is like an untried friend.'

'I am too old to be changing gods,' said Hakon.

Erland's inner laughter had returned to him. 'As to that, there is no need, for you. You are of our old world, passing through. You are not Kievan, not Rus. And even for us, who are both these things, must one desert an old god because one prays from time to time to a New One? I took my Manhood Oath on Thor's Ring before the men in the God-House, but when I was a child in the women's quarters of my father's hall, I sacrificed to the gods of my mother's people. I prayed then to Epona the Great Mare. I pray to her still at foaling time.'

I had guessed already that, like me, he was of mixed blood; with his long bones and thick fair hair that contrasted so oddly with his sallow skin and high flat cheek-bones and those narrow dark eyes. But it was in that moment, when I should have been thinking of the things of the Spirit, there came to me for the first time an awareness of the Rus as a People, not just a southward swarming of the Viking hoards, with the Tribes as a kind of lesser folk in-gathered along the way.

While I was held by this new thought, this new awareness, the talk moved on; and when I began to listen again, the talk of the gods had taken a new turn, to include next spring's war-hosting; and someone was saying that the Christian Faith was not the only thing that the Khan was taking from Byzantium; that despite the old treaty between them, he had demanded as part payment for his help, that he should be given the Emperor's sister, the Princess Anna, for his wife.

I spoke up almost before I knew it, honestly bewildered. 'But if the followers of this—this Muhammad are not allowed to drink wine, a Christian is not allowed more than one wife—and they say that Khan Vladimir has three already.'

Faces turned to me, one of the older men laughed. 'So ha! The one who looks and listens can speak as well! The pup knows how to give tongue!'

Erland said, 'Not to mention the concubines. . . . The Khan is one to make his own laws for his own living. If he has three already, what difference can a fourth make? He will make this one his wife by the rites of the Kristni's church, and for the rest—with so many women in his house, who shall say whether any of the others are wives or no?'

I said stubbornly, 'Then I am sorry for the Princess Anna.'

Under the table, Thormod kicked me hard on the ankle.

There was laughter all up and down the hall, and someone said, 'I'd not let our gentle Khan hear you say so, hound pup!'

Erland said nothing, but his eyes were on my face, a curious long look that I remembered afterward, and he went on making that delicate finger-play with his silken yellow beard. Then abruptly he sat up straight. 'We have had enough of talk, let's call out the sword-dancers.'

10 The Holm Ganging

Next day went for the most part, as the first had done, in getting the *Red Witch* unloaded, her cargo warehoused, and her gear stowed for the winter, and the vessel herself slung in her place in the long ship-shed where Erland Silkbeard's three slim galleys already lay waiting for the spring. At first I was surprised that all that day, as all the day before, Thormod made no move to seek out the two we had come to meet. 'How long do we wait?' I mind asking, almost angrily, for such waiting did not come easily to me, though I have learned the way of it since.

But Thormod, like most of his breed, had a strong sense of fate. He looked up from the cordage that we were stowing, and said matter-of-factly, 'The Norns who spin the lives of men have brought us all four to the same place. As to the time—there's no hurry. First we get the *Red Witch* bedded down for the winter. Plenty of time for the other thing after that. Give me a hand with the rope here.'

There was not much longer to wait, after all, as it happened.

Evening came and all was completed, and we started back for Erland's hall. A crew stripping rotten timbers from a galley further along the boat-strand had made a fire, and a handful of other men had gathered to share it, for the autumn chill was, as Erland had said, already beginning to bite when the sun went down. The men gathered close, and beyond them the Dnieper had the hard grey glint of a sword-blade; and a little knife-edged wind was stirring the coarse grasses above the river-bank shingle. Thormod and I and a few more of the *Red Witch*'s crew strolled over to join them.

And then on the edge of the group, Thormod checked, and I felt him tense in his tracks, felt his hackles rising like a hound's at the smell of wolf. I looked where he was looking, and saw two men standing on the fringe of the firelight. One of them glanced round in the same instant, and touched the other, who turned also.

I saw two broad, steady faces under rough mouse-fair hair, as alike as the faces of two brothers could be, save that one of them— he looked as though he might be a year or so the younger—had a small puckered scar along one cheek-bone. It seemed to me that everyone else had fallen back, leaving the four of us alone with empty space around us. And I knew—even if they had not so clearly been brothers, even if one had not had that small scar on his cheek-bone, I would have known by the kind of silent crackling in the air, that they were the two we had come to meet.

The elder of the two, he that must be Herulf Herulfson, was the first to break the silence. 'You got our message, then.'

'I found it waiting for me beside my father's body,' Thormod said.

'And here is our meeting, after all.'

'After all?'

'We wondered if you might have cast in your lot with the King of Dublin for another year. A year would be long to wait.'

'No, I was home in time for the Arval.' Thormod spoke reasonably, like a friend giving his reasons for being late at an appointed meeting. 'But the *Red Witch* ran into foul weather off Bornholm and we were storm-bound for five days. Maybe even a few days of waiting seem long when the hounds are on one's track.'

'Do you think we feared you, then?' The younger, he with the scar on his cheek, spoke up more hotly than his brother. 'All we feared was that we had come on a fool's trail that you would not follow.'

'Did you not know that I would surely come?' Thormod said. 'Even if it were in another year, another ten years, even if I must clamber out of my grave to follow!'

'That is fine fierce talk. But it did just cross our minds that when you came to think it over, the odds might have seemed too big for your belly; and that would have been a pity.'

'Odds?'

'Two against one,' said the elder brother.

Thormod smiled; at least he bared his teeth. 'A pity indeed. If I had thought the odds too great, it is in my mind that my father's blood would have cried out to me that he went down to the same odds, and without warning.' Suddenly his hand was on my shoulder, gripping so that I felt his fingers grinding into the bone. 'But indeed, the odds are two against two. Anders, Herulf, look well upon Jestyn my blood-brother.'

We looked at each other, across the blue and green flames of the old salty timbers burning. And the sad thing was that we could have liked each other well, if it had not been for the man lying stark in the house-place at Sitricstead with the torches burning at his head and feet.

'So. That is well,' Herulf said at last. 'When shall we settle the matter?'

'Now, if you like,' Thormod said. 'The fire will give us light to see by.'

Herulf shook his head. 'This has been a long trail, it can wait a few hours longer. We are all weary after a day's work. A meal, and sleep, and we shall make a fight of it that will do honour to our fathers.'

'At daybreak, then. What place?'

'The river levels southward shall give us elbow room for our Holm Ganging.'

I had heard something before, of this Viking way of settling a feud. In the old days, I knew, it had been a Holm Ganging, an Island Going, indeed, when two men with a quarrel to the death between them would take themselves to the nearest small island to fight it out. In these days the Fighting Ground is merely a circle marked out with hazel rods; but in these days, still, of two who carry their knives into it, only one comes out alive.

But in this Holm Ganging there would be four of us—and that night, lying under the heavy wolfskin rugs in the hayloft where we slept, I listened while Thormod explained to me the pattern of next morning's fight.

I had thought that we should fight two against two, but it seemed that that was not the way of it.

'Herulf and I are the elder brothers,' said Thormod. 'Therefore to us, is the honour of First Fight. We meet in the hazel circle in single combat, and whichever of us goes down, the other stands back and waits for the second fight to be fought out. Your fight, and Anders', the younger brothers.'

'And then?' I said, speaking muffled into the hay.

'Then, if both of us, or both of them, be ravens' food, the thing is finished. If it be one of them and one of us, then it is for the two left standing to finish it; and when *that* fight is done, then the blood will be cleansed and the debt paid and the feud over.'

'It seems a cold way of fighting out a death quarrel,' I said.

'It is the pattern of the Holm Ganging.' And Thormod turned over, hunching himself for sleep.

I could not sleep, for the coldness that was like a stone in my belly as I lay long and long afterward, listening to Thormod's quiet breathing in the dark beside me, and the rustling of some small live creature in the hay, and wondering how I should be lying that time next night.

Alas, in cold blood, I have never been the stuff of which heroes are forged.

In the wide flat country that spreads about Kiev, one is always aware of the sky; a great bowl of sky arching over the world, with nothing to break its power of brewing up weather, and streaked in autumn and spring with the dark flight-lines of birds going north or south. I mind now, as though it were today's dawn, the high shining steeps of sky, and a wavering arrow-head of wild duck flying over, as Thormod and I went down to next morning's Holm Ganging. I looked up to watch them out of sight, and wondered if I should ever see wild duck against a morning sky again. I had nothing of the Northmen's grim, amused acceptance of fate. I was young, and I wanted to live. I wanted Thormod to live. I wanted other wild duck against other shining morning skies. . . . My blood was very cold.

Word of the feud had gone round, and it seemed that half Kiev had turned out to watch the fight and the kill; and in the midst of them Hakon One-eye and another man who I guessed must be Ship-Chief of the *Serpent*, were marking out the fighting ground with birch branches, there being no hazel in those parts. There were yellow leaves clinging to the twigs, and they fluttered in the light chill wind that brushed through the marsh grasses.

We took our stand on one side of the Fighting Ground, as Anders and Herulf came through the crowd to the other; and the gathered onlookers waited. I felt for the knife in my belt. Above the belt I was naked under my cloak; stripped for battle like the other three; and the wind blew cold, and I could feel nothing, no anger, no hate, for the two men across the Fighting Ground, to fire my blood within me. The feud was mine only because of the little white scar on my wrist, only because it was Thormod's— though that was none so ill a reason, I suppose.

There was no signal, no blowing of horns; only, beside me, Thormod flung off his cloak and stepped forward into the ring of birch branches. And from the far side, in the same instant, Herulf did the same.

For maybe three heartbeats of time, they stood facing each other, knife in hand, while the crews of the *Red Witch* and the *Serpent* and half Kiev behind them crowded close to watch.

Then they began to circle, as hounds circle in the moment before springing at each other's throats. Crouching a little, each trying for the advantage of the low morning light behind him. And again it seemed to me that the crowd melted away like mist, leaving nothing in the world but the space within the circle of birch branches, and the two warily circling figures. Herulf made a feint, then sprang back out of touch, and again the wary circling began. Then Thormod leapt in, and the blades rang together, before Herulf ducked out sideways with Thormod after him. Ah now, but who can remember in all detail the swift fierce patterns of a knife-fight across thirty years? Certain moments stay in the mind, no more. I remember the flash of a knife-blade in the pale marsh-land sunlight, and a roar going up from the crowd as the red blood sprang out from a long gash in Thormod's right forearm. I remember the pad of feet, and the quick hiss of indrawn breath. I remember thinking that Herulf was growing tired—and then, realizing with a sudden sickness in my belly, that he was holding off deliberately, seeking to tire Thormod. Succeeding, too! For even as I watched, it seemed to me that Thormod was growing slower, less sure—unless it was the gash in his forearm. I remember being vaguely aware of the taste of blood in my mouth, though I did not know until later that it was from my own lower lip that I had all but bitten through.

Then it was as though Thormod, aware of that deadly slowing up, gathered himself together and flung all that he had left of strength and speed against his enemy. For a few moments they seemed locked together, reeling to and fro; and then they were on the ground, with Thormod underneath. I saw his left arm flung up to ward off the death-strike; he gave a desperate sideways heave, as Herulf's dagger flashed down, and the crowd roared again as he came uppermost with his left hand gripping the other's dagger-wrist. Oh, I remember all that well enough. I saw them straining together, and felt within myself how their muscles would be cracking and the blood pounding, and the breath panting behind the bared teeth. And then somewhere in the tensed tangle of their bodies there was a convulsive flash of movement; and for a long slow heartbeat of time, no more movement at all. Then, slowly, Thormod got to his feet. Herulf lay still on the reddening ground, with a crimson mouth open and spouting the bright lung-blood under his ribs. But the flow stopped almost at once.

Anders gave one long look to his brother's body, and then no more, as men came to haul it from the Fighting Ground. Thormod came out through the ring of birch branches, breathing fast, and changing his knife into his left hand while he rubbed the right on his breeks, trying to wipe away the slipperiness of the blood trickling down his forearm.

We had time to exchange one look, no time for any word; and then Anders tossed off his cloak and drew his dagger from his belt, and stepped forward into the Fighting Circle.

I dropped my own cloak and kicked it behind me, and went to meet him. And standing face to face, I saw, as I had not seen in last night's firelight, that his eyes were of odd colours, as Orm had said, one blue and the other grey. Already our hands were hovering on the edge of movement above the knives in our belts, a moment more and they would have been out. But in that moment a voice broke the waiting silence of the crowd. A voice clearly used to giving orders and having them obeyed. 'Break! Break off, I say!'

There was a ruffle of voices, and a falling back to let someone through; and turning with the rest, I saw a man on a tiger-spot horse come riding through the cleared way.

On the edge of the Fighting Ground he reined in, and sat his fidgeting beast, looking down at Anders and me. A big man, though broad rather than tall, with a face that seemed to have been made in a hurry, the nose crooked, one pale bright eye set a little higher than the other, a big mouth made for savage laughter and overfull of strong yellow teeth. He wore rough woollen breeks and a goatskin jerkin with the hair inside making a dark ragged fringe at the edges; but his boots were of fine soft saffron-coloured leather, and under the rough jerkin a glint of gold showed at his throat. It seemed that he had been setting out for a day's sport, for the knot of hearth companions behind him carried hawks—he carried a magnificent gyr falcon on his own gloved fist—or had hounds coupled in leash. I had not seen him before, but I knew without doubting, by his air of riding head and shoulders taller than other men, that this was Khan Vladimir.

His curious light eyes flickered from Anders to me, to Thormod who had come to stand with us, to the long shape of Herulf lying still under his cloak at the side of the Fighting Ground, and back again. 'So; it has been a good Holm Ganging, and now it is ended.'

Anders gave him back look for look. 'A good Holm Ganging, Lord, but it is not yet ended.'

The Khan smiled; a smile to make the hairs lift on the back of one's neck. 'It is easy to see that you are strange-come to these parts. When you know me better, all three of you, my heroes, you will know that when Khan Vladimir says that the Holm Ganging is ended, the Holm Ganging is ended, as the night follows the day.'

There was a small silence, and then Thormod spoke, his voice at its most level. 'There is Blood Feud between Anders Herulfson and us two. Not even the Lord of Kiev is above the laws of the Blood Feud, only the gods.'

'At most times, I would grant you that,' said Vladimir, with the air of a reasonable man. 'But the call has gone out for War Hosting, and in time of Ravens' Gatherings, all else waits.'

'Lord, there can be no War Hosting until the spring,' Thormod said.

'The War Hosting began in the hour when I seized the *Serpent* to serve with the War Fleet when the time comes. It is quite simple—softly, softly now, jewel of my heart!' (This to the falcon, who was growing restless as though she felt the stress like thunder in the air about her.) 'You will swear to me on that which you hold sacred, to leave this feud lying, until the fighting in the south be done and the War Host disbanded, or you will spend the winter in chains. The choice is yours. I have too good a use for fighting men to be wasteful of them now.'

'Lord,' Thormod seemed to have become the spokesman for the three of us, 'we deny your right—'

Vladimir made a sound at the back of his throat; a kind of coughing snarl like a mountain lion. 'My right! Was it not told to you two nights since, that I make my own right? Even to the number of my wives before the throne of the White Kristni?' His eye was on me at that moment, and I kept my head up to meet it, but my stomach knotted with fear. I saw the laughter in his pale bright glance, but it might be the laughter of the God behind the thunderbolt, and I was not reassured.

It was then that I remembered how Erland Silkbeard had looked at me, two nights since, and it seemed to me that it had been an enemy's look. But like enough it saved all our lives, for that time.

'So,' said Khan Vladimir. 'Will you swear? Or will you pass the winter chained like hounds in the palace forecourt?'

The three of us looked at each other. And I heard the little wind through the marsh grasses, and the stir and rustle of the crowd, and a horse ruckling down its nose. Then Anders quoted softly, "Keep a stone in your pocket seven years for your enemy, take it out and turn it and keep it seven more, then take it out and throw." There is no hurry; and I am thinking that none of us three will forget, if we live to see the end of the fighting in the south.'

Thormod had turned back to the Khan. 'Since it seems that in one way or another way, the thing must wait, whether we swear or no, and since we would spend the winter out of chains—on what shall we swear?' Suddenly and unexpectedly, his level voice had that glint of laughter. 'On Thor's Ring?'

The Khan's mouth widened at the corners, over the strong yellow teeth. 'That is a question, to be sure. Not on Thor's Ring, no. You and you, on your father's graves.' His gaze flickered between Thormod and Anders, then passed on to me, consideringly. 'You, on this—' And he thrust a hand into the breast of his jerkin and pulled out a heavy cross of rough gold set with turquoise that blazed in the morning sun.

So the three of us swore; and the Blood Feud was laid by until the fighting in the south should be over; and we turned ourselves to the coming winter.

And Herulf Herulfson, his part in it played out and finished for all time, was home-lain in the rich black earth of the Kiev marshes.

11 Viking Wind

The fires of the maples burned themselves out, and the Dnieper froze over, and soon the Kiev marshes were deep in snow that drifted before the blizzard winds. It was warm within doors, where the fires of wood and cattle-dung were kept blazing day and night. And from outside, you could see the patches of melted snow round the smoke-holes in the roofs. But out of doors the cold, striking through hide breeks and jerkin and thick wadmal cloak from the slop kist in Erland's hall (we of the *Red Witch* counted as Erland's men now, his food in our bellies, his clothes for our backs), was like no cold that I had ever felt before.

Autumn, and the more open days of winter, was a time of tree-felling in the forest land north of the city; and the trunks were roped and dragged down by oxen, and stacked above the keel strand to weather as much as might be before the shipbuilding that would come with the first days of spring.

And speaking for myself, I got to seeing the steam rising from the nostrils of the straining oxen and hearing the crack of the long whips in my sleep.

'A green fleet,' said Hakon One-eye. 'But if it holds together as far as Miklagard, we can have vessels of gold and cedar to carry us home again.'

All winter long we worked in the boat-sheds, Thormod and Anders and I, with the rest, re-fitting vessels already there, renewing blocks and tackle, pitching sides and re-caulking seams. All winter the rope-walk was busy, and from the town above came the ding of hammer on anvil, where the armourer smiths were at work mending old weapons and forging new; while, in the Khan's palace and the fire-halls of his nobles, the women gathered to stitch the wadmal sails and work the spread-winged raven banners as women have done in the north whenever the Viking Kind gather for war.

So the winter passed; longer and colder than any winter of our old world; dragging on and on, the cold seeming to grow more bitter as the days lengthened, until it was hard to believe that spring would ever come again to the frozen white wastes that stretched from the world's end to the world's end.

But at last a day came when the wind went round to the south and there was a different smell in it, and the cattle grew restive in their yards, under the cloud of their steaming breath. By next morning it had gone round to the north again, and there was a blizzard, and spring seemed as far away as ever. But in a few days more, the icicles began to lengthen under the eaves; and one night in the sleeping-lodge behind Erland's Hall, I woke to a sound like the cracking of a bull-whip. I rolled over and kicked Thormod, but Thormod was already awake. 'It will be the ice going,' he said.

And a Kievan on the other side of the lodge added, 'There'll be clear water from here down to the Inland Sea in a few days' time.'

Spring in the land of the Rus proved to be a wet and muddy time. The blocks of broken ice piled up and dammed the Dnieper, so that soon there were floods all across the marshes; and for a while, the world that had been frozen under white snow seemed foundering in black mud. But it was spring! Pipits flittered among the alders along the river-bank that were suddenly frithy with dark catkins. The long-ships were run out from the high-crested keel-sheds down on to the slipways. And the ship-building that had begun with timber felling in the autumn got into full swing, so that all day long the waterside of Kiev rang with shipyard sounds: adze on timber, hammer on anvil, the shovelling of great fires that steamed the light planks into shape for the sides of the new vessels. And everywhere was the smell of pitch and new timber and the sharp tang of burning cattle-dung, and the green freshness of the spring.

And spring passed into summer: a dry hot summer of dust

blowing in from the steppes, and quick-piling thunderstorms; and for a little while there were nightingales, and brief bright dusty flowers, cornflowers and crimson poppies along the edges of the barley.

Back in the early spring the messengers had begun to come and go, riding the small sturdy tarpan, the half-wild ponies of the Steppes, carrying the Khan's summons the length and breadth of the Rus country. And soon, from all directions, by boat down the waterways that fed into the Dnieper, and on horseback raising the summer dust behind them, the fighting men began to gather; while long-ship after long-ship came sweeping down-river from the north, bringing fresh Viking crews from the Baltic shores, eager for the fighting and the promise of gold that our northbound friends of the Great Portage must have shouted broadcast.

While it was still early summer, another Embassy came up from Miklagard; two of the great red-painted naval galleys of Byzantium; one of them clearly the escort, while on board the other, a little group of men in rich light cloaks as gaily coloured as flower petals, held themselves proudly aloof on the afterdeck.

I mind looking up from a rope that I was splicing, to see them come, and asking of the world in general, 'Could it be that they are bringing the Princess?'

Orm, who was working beside me, laughed. 'They're businessmen, the Byzantines, they don't pay until the payment has been earned.'

'They'll be here to see why we haven't come yet,' said someone else.

'Na, na, they'll know that it takes time to raise six thousand fighting men and the ships to carry them. Just to see how the thing goes.'

And watching them come up-river at racing speed, the rowers tossing up their oars at the last instant, so that they slid alongside the jetty under their own way, Thormod said, 'Yon was well done! These men of Miklagard are seamen in their own fashion.'

Orm nodded, his eyes screwed up against the sun-dazzle off the water. 'Though I'm thinking 'twould be interesting to see how they would handle a keel in Sumburgh Roost at ebbtide.'

As summer went by, the low ground around Kiev became an armed camp; and ship after ship went down the slipways; and all along the strand up and down-river of the city the long keels lay like basking sea-beasts, old and flank-scarred by many voyages, young and green-timbered with their first seafaring yet ahead of them. And still the weapon smiths worked on, forging the great two-handed swords and the war axes of the Viking Kind.

At last, with the late summer drying out in grey dust and the first sparks of another autumn already showing here and there among the maples, close on a year after the *Red Witch* came down-river into Kiev, close on a year after the unfinished Holm Ganging, all was ready, men trained and armed, ships fitted for sailing.

On the last day, there was a great service held in the church of the White Kirstni, long since finished, to pray for the victory of the Viking fleet—and for the victory of Byzantium over the rebels, but that was an afterthought.

In the old dark God-House above the boat-strand, men gathered also, the men who had come down that summer from the north, the crews of the ships that did not belong to Kiev and therefore were not bound to the Khan's new faith.

I went to the God-House with the crew of the *Red Witch*.

It was not easy for me, the choice; and I lay awake most of the night before, pulled now this way and now that, between two loyalties. But when the great bronze bell that we had hauled up the hill through rejoicing crowds to the new church in the spring, sounded its call to Christian Kiev, I did not answer it.

Many of those who went with Khan Vladimir to fill the church and crowd the open space around it, would be down at the God-House later, I knew; as Erland Silkbeard had said, one need not desert the old gods because one occasionally prayed to a new one; the Viking Kind can always make room for another god, having several of their own to start with. But I could not do that, having only one to start with. So I went away and sat on the shore where the wild birds were calling, and prayed, all the same, with my face in my hands. 'Dear God, I do not ask you to forgive me, only to believe that there isn't any other way.'

And when the day faded into the dusk, and the Viking Kind came down with their torches, I got up and went and joined them.

The Leaders and the Ship-Chiefs went inside; the rest of us, for whom there was no room, crowded before the door, in the russet light of the torches and the white light of a waning moon. We heard the dying bleat of the goat, and saw the priest come out to daub the blood on the dragon-carved doorposts, and took the oath on Thor's Ring that he held up for us to see, to maintain the War-Brotherhood until the Host should be disbanded. And standing there beside Thormod, I looked across and saw Anders in the crowd, and met his gaze, as if it were waiting for mine. We had kept the vow for almost a year already, letting the feud lie fallow. But now? How much longer? A few weeks? A few months? I wished again that I could feel this long-drawn quarrel as my own; that I could have the anger in my belly to warm the waiting. And now I had prayed to strange gods, and so in all likelihood I was damned. But I wasn't wasting time regretting that, it was just a fact. I was Thormod's shoulder-to-shoulder man, Thormod's follower wherever he went; and I supposed I could face damnation with Thormod if I had to; assuredly I could not leave him to face it alone. It was simply, as I had explained to my own God, that there wasn't any other way.

The torches shifted, and I lost Anders among the crowding shadows.

Next day we ran the ships down the keel-strand and the southward voyage began. Squadron after squadron, we went, each following our own Raven—Erland's, it was said, had golden hairs from his own beard stitched into its eyes and beak and talons— all following the great black-winged banner of Khan Vladimir. And so we headed down the Dnieper; close on two hundred longships in all; six thousand men of the Rus and the north, sweeping down the Viking wind, to the aid of the Golden Emperor in his golden city.

Orm, who had a knack with such things, made a song about it, and we sang it as we swung to the oars.

> Here we come with the wind behind us,
> Lift her! Lift her!
> A long pull for Miklagard.
> The wind in our sails and the oar-thresh flying,
> A strong pull for Miklagard.

Emperor in your Golden City,
Lift her! Lift her!
A long pull for Miklagard.
Look to the north and see us coming,
A strong pull for Miklagard.

You shouted for help, and help we are bringing,
Lift her! Lift her!
A long pull for Miklagard.
Our arms are strong and our sword-blades singing,
A strong pull for Miklagard.

First the fighting and then the pay,
Lift her! Lift her!
A long pull for Miklagard.
Gift-gold you promised at close of the day,
A strong pull for Miklagard.

Here on the wind we come, Northman and Rus,
Lift her! Lift her!
A long pull for Miklagard.
Nothing to fear now, Little Emperor,
A strong pull for Miklagard,
Nothing to fear now, excepting *us*!

It was really a very bad song, I suppose, it did not even rhyme
properly, and after a while as we got further south, it seemed
better to change it here and there; but it pleased us well enough
at the time.

12 Battle for Abydos

I suppose no man who has once seen Constantinople ever forgets that first sight. For me—for us—it came in the honey-coloured light of an early autumn evening, as we swarmed ashore from the Golden Horn, with half the city, as it seemed, turned out to greet us. I remember city walls that seemed to have been built for a fortress of giants, tall buildings set about with cypress trees and roofed with russet and purple, gold and green, vast arches upheld on marble columns that twisted as fantastically as bindweed stems, towers that seemed straining up to touch the sky and great aqueducts that strode across the city on legs of white stone. I remember little fretted balconies that clung like swallows' nests high overhead to the walls of tall narrow houses; and wide streets that opened into gardens and open spaces where statues of marble heroes and golden saints and bronze horsemen stood tall and proud among shade-trees; and everywhere the domes of Christian churches catching the last of the run-honey light. I, who thought that I knew cities because I had seen Dublin and Kiev, had never imagined that there could be such a city in the world of men.

Later, it became a city in which real people lived and died, where one could buy melons or have one's boots re-soled, with barracks and wine-shops as well as palaces, and children playing on doorsteps, and evil smells, and dark alleys where it was not wise to go without a friend so that you could cover each other's backs if need be. But to this day, the city that I saw on that first evening remains in my memory a city in a crowded dream.

The camp outside the great walls of Theodosius, where we slept under tents of striped ships' canvas in the months that followed, was much closer to the world I knew.

We had expected to be unleashed at once against the Emperor's enemies, whose watch-fires flowered in the darkness every night, clear across the narrow waters of the Bosphorus; but instead, we spent the autumn months training with the Imperial Guards.

'Patience, children,' said Erland Silkbeard, when some of us grew restive, 'no War Host can fight its best when its two halves have not learned to fight together and know nothing of each other's ways of warfare.'

'But meanwhile, time goes by,' grumbled Hakon Ship-Chief.

'Surely. But that's no matter. The Emperor has one advantage —besides that he has our swords behind him—his Red Ships hold the seas, and so long as they do that, he can afford to wait, and choose his own fighting-time. Also'—he was playing gently with his beard, much as a man gentling the neck-feathers of his falcon— 'the Byzantines know that the men of the north seldom make war in the winter; so when the last leaves are off the almond trees, these rebel Byzantines will lower their guards, at least a little. That is when we strike.'

Aye, and on a winter's night, with snow to aid us, we struck.

Led by Basil himself, the whole War Host—us, that is, and the Guards; the rest of the Emperor's troops were still in Thrace— were ferried across the Bosphorus under cover of flurrying snow. And in the dark just before dawn we descended on Chrysopolis while the rebels were still asleep.

I had looked ahead to that fight, while it still lay in the future, with an odd mingling of feelings, with little cold queazes in the pit of my stomach when I woke in the night, but also with an eagerness that I had caught from Thormod and the rest; for to the Northmen, fighting is almost like love, a kind of flowering of life. But when it came, there was no true fight, only a messy and undignified slaughter of half-awakened men before they could reach for their weapons. Oh, I played my part with the rest, my sword drank its share of blood and filth. . . . Hardly a man escaped us. Bardas Phocas himself was some otherwhere, gathering more troops, but his leaders were crucified on the spot. The whole night's work left a foul taste in the mouth. . . .

After Chrysopolis was lost to him, Bardas Phocas took his newly-gathered troops and headed south for Abydos, the Customs port, where the Emperor's dues were exacted from the Corn Fleet passing up and down the long narrows that men call the Hellespont. He laid siege to the fort; I suppose he had some thought of using the corn-ships to get his troops across to link up with the Bulgars in Thrace; and some such plan might have worked, if the Red Ships had not held command of the sea. As it was, they relieved Abydos almost at once, while we of the War Host followed our little square-set Emperor down the coast, to raise the siege.

And now again, we saw their line of watch-fires in the night; but with no Bosphorus between us and them, only a few hundred paces of sandy scrub. And they were ready and waiting for us, and the fight that was coming with the morning would not be like Chrysopolis; not like Chrysopolis at all.

It was a spring night, but the light wind brushing through the tamarisk scrub had still an edge to it after dark, and we huddled close about the camp fires, feeding them with dry branches, long after we had eaten the evening food. We had ceased to be a fleet, and become a land army over the past few months; but old ships' crews still had a way of hanging together, and most of us from the *Red Witch* had gathered to the same fire, and sat companionably going over our gear, the mail-shirts and nut-shaped helmets that made us look much like any other of the Byzantine front-line troops, and making ready our weapons against tomorrow. And rubbing away at my sword-blade, I thought suddenly that if we won his battle for him, and the Emperor had no more need of his Viking War Host, and we were paid off, and free of the oath taken in the Kiev marshes. . . . But maybe we should just be dead. Tomorrow night would be time enough to start worrying about the old feud again. . . . I rubbed harder at the blade; and my hand slipped and I gashed my thumb on the keen edge. It was only a small cut, but the blood sprang out dark in the firelight, and I cursed and sucked it.

Orm laughed. 'Jestyn is so eager for tomorrow's fight that he must start blooding his blade already!'

Hakon cocked his one eye from the new strap he was fixing on his shield. 'At least tomorrow is like to give us work in hotter blood than we found at Chrysopolis.'

'Chrysopolis was a shore-killing,' I said, scowling at my gashed thumb.

'So—but the pickings were good.' Orm shook the chain hung with little silver pomegranates that he wore about his neck.

And Thormod said with that familiar edge of laughter in his voice, 'You'd better not wear that into battle tomorrow, old bell-weather, or they'll hear you coming and single you out a mile away.'

There was a snatch of laughter round the fire; but a long sough of wind came shivering up through the tamarisks, and somewhere a dog howled.

Morning swallowed the watch-fires; and the walls of Abydos that had been a low black cliff behind the enemy camp, shone dusty pale against the deepening blue of the sky. We had eaten bread and raisins, and prayed to our different gods, as men pray in the dawn before the battle. And we stood ready, drawn up in fighting-line along the dunes. The light wind that had hushed through the shore scrub all night, stirred the blue and purple standards of the Guards, and spread the black raven banners above our ranks. And across the open ground, the coloured flicker of enemy standards answered them.

The Emperor had come out from his tent to pray with his troops for victory. And now, with his standard-bearer and his staff officers about him, and his brother Constantine at his side, he came riding the length of our battle-line. Square and short-legged on a horse too big for him—he always rode horses too big for him in his younger days; but he could handle them as though he and they were one. Standing in the second rank of Erland Silkbeard's following, I watched the sacred standard draw near, the figure of the Virgin embroidered on it jewelled and brilliant in the cool morning light, her cloth-of-gold halo catching the first rays of the sun in an answering sunburst. It drew level with our black-winged ravens, then passed on. And in its passing, all along the ranks of the Imperial Army, it left a wake of silence; the silence that comes in the last moments before battle. Only, above the heavy drubbing of my own heart, I heard from the cavalry wings the jink of a bridle as a horse here and there fidgeted and tossed its head, smelling the coming fight.

Between the helmets of the two men in front of me, I could see where the glittering banner of Bardas Phocas flew above the small tump of higher ground on which he had taken up his position. I could see the shimmer of movement among the dark knot of horsemen surrounding it, and one among them—it must have been Phocas himself by the white plume in his helmet—came pricking out from the rest. I thought I saw his arm go up; another instant and the trumpets would be yelping, the whole rebel line spilling forward to the charge.

And then something happened—we heard later that a quail, sitting tight on her nest among the scrub until the last possible moment, had got up almost under the hooves of the rebel leader's horse. From our lines we could not make out the details, but we heard the quail's alarm-call; and saw the sudden tumult of horses flinging this way and that under the rebel standard.

'Someone's been thrown,' Thormod said, and caught his breath. 'It's Phocas himself by the look of things! Thor's Hammer! what an omen for his men to follow!'

I had my eyes screwed up, reaching into the distance. 'Looks as though he's up again.'

'Someone's bringing him another horse,' Orm put in.

All along the battle-line the murmur ran.

Then from the little group out in front of us where Basil sat his horse under the Imperial Standard, a bare blade flashed down in the morning sun; and all up and down the battle-lines, the trumpets sounded and were answered; royal and rebel Byzantine trumpets and our own booming war-horns shouting against each other like fighting-cocks at dawn. For a long heartbeat of time, both armies seemed held on the edge of movement, like wine rising on the rim of a tilted cup before it spills over; and then we moved forward. I remember the tightening in my belly, and putting one foot before the other, and knowing that the waiting was over and the thing had begun.

Between the heads of the front rank I could see the rebel standard, the moving ranks, the dust already beginning to curl up, and through the dust, the white helmet-plume of their leader. I could see also that something was hideously amiss with Bardas Phocas; the white plume was swaying from side to side, more and more widely as it drew nearer, until suddenly —and nothing startled the horse this time—he flung out his arms and pitched from the saddle.

There was a kind of faltering, a break in rhythm, in the rebel ranks. Phocas's bodyguard came spurring forward to cover him and get him away; and in the same instant the Emperor's sword flashed again in the sun, and we heard his voice, loud as any trumpet—even now that he is old he has the kind of voice a Ship-Chief might envy—shouting for the charge.

We burst forward like hounds slipped from the leash. We crashed into the enemy battle-line before they had time to steady again, and hurled their front rank back into the ranks behind. I heard afterwards that our men broke clear through at that first charge, and turned about to thrust home again from the rear, cutting the enemy into separate, ragged clots of men to be cut down piecemeal. I heard that the rebels fought stubbornly; but that one moment of uncertainty when their leader went down made sure of their defeat.

But at the time, all I knew of that battle before Abydos—all, I am thinking, that most men except the leaders ever do know of a battle—was a confusion of trampling and shouting and weapon-ring and choking dust all about me; and the widened eyes of the man who was going to kill me unless I first killed him, glaring at me across our shield-rims, and the snake-dart of a spear past my cheek, and somewhere the scream of a wounded horse; and the fighting-smell of blood at the back of my nose.

All the formless tumult of a dream; and only one thing real—the steadying consciousness of Thormod's shoulder somewhere alongside mine.

13 Faces by Firelight

The Emperor did not sleep in Abydos that night. He was always a man more at home in an armed camp than within city walls, and always a man to bide with his men. So while Constantine went off in search of city comforts, he spent the night after the battle as he had spent the night before it, in his great blue and purple tent pitched beside a few oleander trees in the midst of the camp.

And for our part in the day's fighting, he ordered that we, the Northmen of Kiev, should furnish his guard for the night.

And how it came about, I'd not be knowing—maybe it was because Erland Silkbeard was the closest and most powerful of Khan Vladimir's Hearth-Companions and Hakon One-Eye an old friend of Erland's—the crew of the *Red Witch* were among the chosen Northmen. Which is how I, who seemed born to spend my life herding cattle in the west of England, stood my guard over the Emperor of Byzantium on the night that he was made safe on his throne.

Every detail of that night stands clear in my mind. Did I not say that I was very young? So young, even for my nineteen years, that it seemed to me a great and glorious thing to stand guard over an Emperor. I remember the sounds of the camp; passing footsteps, a voice upraised in a snatch of song. And beyond the camp sounds, I was aware of a great silence that was the silence of the spent battlefield, pricked now and again by the cry of some night-prowling beast that had smelt blood and come to the feasting. There were torches everywhere, down at the picket lines, before the tents of the generals; distant cressets flowering small and red above the ramparts of Abydos; and scattered through the camp, the watch-fires, and the darkness between, full of the shifting shadows of men lost and found and lost again as they came and went their ways. I was standing beside the entrance to the Royal Tent, leaning on my sword, and staring into the glow of the watch-fire where those of us not yet standing sentry sat or sprawled, talking low-voiced or already asleep.

Someone came crosswise out of the dark into the firelight, and glanced down in passing at the sleepers huddled in their cloaks. He checked the merest breath of time, his gaze caught by one in particular, and then was gone again into the dark, on his way to wherever it was that he was going. But it seemed to me that I could still see his face: Anders Herulfson's face, firelit against the night; and I looked where he had looked in that brief, passing moment, knowing what—who—I should see.

Thormod was sleeping on his back with his face tipped to the sky, his cloak pulled close about him; and suddenly, piercingly, I remembered the one time that I had seen his father lying so, with the brown bearskin pulled to his chin, and the torches burning at his head and feet. And the hair rose on the back of my neck.

Last night, I had wondered how long it would be before the War Host was disbanded. But tonight, with the Emperor safe on his throne, the thought leapt out at me with more of urgency, more of cold menace, making my heart race and the palms of my hands grow wet. For one moment it was even in my mind that when they changed the guard I might slip away instead of lying down by the fire, and go hunting. . . . My knife-blade under his ribs in some dark corner of the camp, and the long-drawn feud would be over, and Thormod safe from it. That would make me an oath-breaker, a faith-breaker, and among the Northmen, nothing that lives is quite so low as the man who breaks faith with his own people. But I do not think it was that that held me back; it was the cold hard certainty that the thing was not mine to do, that if I were Thormod, and someone, even my blood-brother, took it into his hands to finish my feud, keeping me safe from it as though I were a child, I would not forgive him, nor count him ever again as my shoulder-to-shoulder man.

So the hideous moment passed.

All the while, I had been aware of the rise and fall of voices from the tent behind me; and suddenly the entrance curtain was thrust aside, and squinting out of the tail of my eye, I saw the Emperor himself come out, and with him the huge square bulk of Khan Vladimir.

Basil stood in his usual position, his hands on his hips and his feet planted well apart, with the air of a man who has come out for a breath of fresh air before he lies down to sleep. And the light of the watch-fire made a russet glow on his round face and magnificent ram's-horn moustache, as he stood rocking a little on his heels and gazing up at the stars.

'This is a good night,' he said, 'a good night after a great day! God delivered the rebels into our hands, striking down their leader in the moment of his impious advance against us. The prisoners who were questioned said that he was dead when he hit the ground.'

After a winter spent in and around Constantinople, I had picked up quite a bit of 'Soldiers' Greek' and could understand most of what they said.

Vladimir nodded. 'Aye; but that was the second time. I'm thinking he must have come down on his head and broken something when yon quail startled his horse.'

'And can you not see the hand of God in that? You do not yet think truly as a Christian, my friend. Why should the Almighty trouble to send a thunderbolt out of a clear sky, when a quail sitting tight on her eggs until the last moment will serve His purpose just as well?' The Emperor was always a practical man as well as a devout one.

'A quail sitting tight on her eggs. And six thousand Northmen also,' said Khan Vladimir.

The Emperor gave a short sharp bellow of laughter, and brought his hand up to grip on the Khan's shoulder, and his gaze down from the stars to look round at the camp fires and the men sleeping or on guard about him. 'Nay, I do not forget your six thousand barbarians! That is why they furnish my guard tonight. A Barbarian Guard.' (But of course he used the Greek form—Varangian. A Varangian Guard. It is a name that has won some fame for itself in the years since then.)

He was silent a while, gazing out over the camp, thoughtfully twiddling the ends of his moustache in the way that he had, then turned to look up at our savage old Northern Bear standing beside him. He said abruptly, 'Brother, I am minded to have a Varangian Guard indeed! When the time comes that you fly north with the wild geese, will you leave me, say, a thousand of your young men, to carry their swords in my service?'

'My young men are free, as the wild geese are free.' I could catch the flash of the Khan's strong yellow teeth in the firelight. 'They would not be the first of the Viking breed to sell their swords for gold and a little glory. If you want them, ask; but ask of themselves, not me.'

'So, I will surely ask. And I will ask of themselves.' His hand still on Vladimir's shoulder, the Emperor turned back into the smoky torch-lit tent, and the entrance curtain fell across behind him.

And almost in the same moment, the trumpets sounded for the second watch of the night, and the whole camp stirred into quiet movement, as one watch took over from the other. All round our fire, men were scrambling to their feet, stretching and making sure that sword sat loose in sheath, stirring with a friendly toe a comrade who had not roused at the trumpet call. There were many who slept like the dead that night, for the fighting had been hot while it lasted; and I have noticed often that after battle, men sleep like the dead, or do not sleep at all.

Orm was suddenly before me, grinning. 'Wake up, Cub, you're asleep on your feet.'

I was not; but I lurched on my stiffened legs when I tried to move, suddenly so weary that everything seemed unreal. 'Drunk again,' said Orm, cheerfully. I stumbled over to where Thormod, whose turn would not come till the third watch, still lay. He had scarcely woken for the trumpets; but I mind that as I pitched down beside him, he muttered something and turned a little towards me, pillowing his head on his arm.

Lying like that, he no longer had the look of his father. The light of the fire was warm on his face, and the little sea wind ruffled his hair like tawny feathers. And he slept now as a living man sleeps. And obscurely, I was comforted, and could not remember quite what my fear had been about.

14 The Varangian Guard

Bardas Schlerus, he that had been Commander of Asia, was out of his rock-hewn prison within a few days of Bardas Phocas's defeat, and collecting troops from the Eastern frontiers, to make his own bid for the Imperial Diadem. So we spent the rest of that spring and summer, while the hills turned tawny as a hound's coat, and the watercourses dried up, hunting him up and down Anatolia, sweating our guts out to bring him to battle before he was strong enough to stand a chance against us. No, hunting is the wrong word, unless men can hunt a marshlight. . . .

And then at summer's end, he sent to the Emperor, asking for terms. The reason was simple enough: he had taken some sickness of the eyes while he was in prison, and was going blind. Assuredly, God was on the side of the Emperor.

Basil was generous. He could be generous in his young days. Sometimes he can, even now. There were no executions; troops who returned to their old loyalties were pardoned and received back, even the leaders. At the time, most men thought that crazy. But the Emperor knew what he was about; for some of his best officers were among them. And to Bardas Schlerus, besides a pardon, he gave one of the smaller of the royal estates in Bithynia to live on, and his old title of Commander of Asia back again—empty, to be sure, like a cup after the wine has been poured away.

He received his old enemy's submission at a banquet in the house that he had just given him. One of the Guard, who was there, told me that he should never forget seeing the old man brought in, stooping a little, but not humbled, his hand on the shoulder of the officer who acted as his guide; and how the Emperor sat in a golden chair of state at the head of the hall, to watch him come, and laughed, and said, 'To think this is the fellow I feared might grab my throne! Now he has to be led to my feet!'

Well, as I say, he had been generous. I suppose even an Emperor's generosity has its limits.

So the summer's campaigning was over. It had not been at all what I had expected when we ran the keels down the Kiev ship-strand and headed south to carry our swords in the Emperor's service; and I'm thinking I was not alone in that. By early autumn we were back in camp below the great walls of Miklagard; and the Viking War Host was paying off and disbanding and scattering to the four winds of the seas. Some of us were following Khan Vladimir north again. There would be just time to make Kiev and the lands round about, before the ice closed in. Some were pushing on into the Mediterranean for a winter of trading with maybe a flourish of piracy thrown in, before heading for the Baltic again in the spring.

And a thousand of us were biding where we were, to carry our swords in the Emperor's service still; for Basil had meant what he said to Khan Vladimir that night outside Abydos, concerning his new Varangian Guard.

And this was the way of it.

Only a few days after we returned to camp, his heralds came. Three men riding into the camp on fine Thessalian stallions, the dust curling up behind them, and talked long with Khan Vladimir in his great tent, while the grooms walked their horses up and down outside. We had an idea what it might be about, and those of us who were most interested looked at each other and began to drift in towards the open space in front of the Khan's lodgement, even before the Horn-of-Gathering sounded.

'So, so, it seems the Emperor has some word to say that concerns all of us,' said Hakon One-Eye.

The heralds came out from the Khan's tent, and remounted their horses; but not, as yet, to ride away. One of them heeled his horse out a little from the other two, as we thrust forward about them, and sat looking us over. He was a smallish thickset man, perched up on a raking horse, and so closely muffled in his dark hooded cloak that even the upper part of his face was hidden. He flung up his hand for silence, and began to speak in the Soldiers' Greek that most of us understood well enough by that time, and in a voice that reached clear through the War Host—

'These are the words of the Emperor Basil and the Emperor Constantine, who sit secure on their throne now that this fighting summer is ended, and who know the worth of good fighting men. To those of you who wish now to go about your own business, they add their thanks to the gold that has already been paid, and wish fair winds and sharp swords. To any among you who wish to remain in their service, they have this to say—that they are minded to form a new personal bodyguard of a thousand men, drawn from those who followed the Prince Vladimir from the north, last year.'

There was a ragged splurge of voices, for the men of the north are not used to listening to their betters in respectful silence—which is maybe because they do not think any man their better.

'A Varangian Guard,' I said to Thormod. 'Did I not tell you?'

And someone shouted, 'Would the pay be worth the pouching?'

The herald laughed—a short sharp bellow of laughter that seemed to me oddly familiar. 'One and a half gold bezants a month, the same as the rest of the Guard's pouch. Richer loot in time of war, for I doubt if any Byzantine soldier can hold his own with the Viking Kind in the art of looting.'

There was a roar of answering laughter, and shouts of 'We're your men!'

'The Emperor's Men,' shouted the herald, when the hubbub died down. He gestured to one of his fellows, who brought a bag from under his cloak and untied the neck. 'A shield here!' the herald called, and when one was brought, and held up like a great dish, the man poured whatever was in the bag into it, pale and rattling like giant hailstones.

'Those aren't golden bezants,' someone shouted.

'They are one thousand knucklebones,' returned the hooded herald. 'They will bide here before your Prince's tent, and any man who would carry a sword in the Emperor's new Guard, let him come up and take his knucklebone, as he would do in his own land when taking service with a new ship. Tomorrow in the

Hippodrome at noon, the Varangian Guard will swear allegiance
to their Emperor.'

'Shall we have a man of our own to Captain us?' someone shouted
from the back of the crowd. 'Or take our orders from a southerner?'

'A man of your own to Captain you. Above and beyond him
you will take no orders from any General of the Army, but only
from the Emperor himself.'

'And who then for our Captain?'

The question was caught up and echoed through the War Host.

Erland Silkbeard strolled out from among the nobles and stood
beside the heralds. He had flung on a loose gown of striped silk
like the slim wild tulips of these parts, and his hair and beard
shone barley fair in the sunlight, made all the paler by the darkness
of his face and the slim hands resting on his sword hilt. 'Erland
Silkbeard, if you will so have it.'

And we would so have it, for that year past we had found him
to be a leader worth the following; as hard as any sea king, despite
his silken ways, fierce as a mountain cat, one who could be merci-
less to his own men, but in the end would stand by them to the
last barricade. So we set up a shout for Erland Silkbeard and a
shout for the Emperor; and as the heralds wheeled their horses
and clattered out of the camp, some of our lads were already spilling forward to take their knucklebones from the shield before
Khan Vladimir's tent.

I mind looking after the three riders in their dark cloaks, and
thinking, Thormod and Orm beside me, thinking, it seemed, the
same thing.

'It would be beneath the Emperor's dignity to come beating up
a following himself like a sea-roving chieftain,' Orm said at last.

I was not so sure. 'He said, the night after we freed Abydos,
that he would ask. Khan Vladimir said if he wanted us, he must
ask it of ourselves, and he said he would. . . .'

'A big horse, that one was riding, for a smallish man,' Thormod
said consideringly. 'couldn't see much of his face under that
cloak, but I'd swear there was only one moustache like that in all
Miklagard. I'm not thinking any herald would use that kind of
blunt soldiers' tongue—and he forgot, and started to leave the
Emperor Constantine out of it, half-way through. No herald would
have done that.'

Someone in the crowd started to sing:

> 'Nothing now to fear, little Emperor,
> Nothing now to fear but US!'

and the laughter and the singing spread, and more and more men began going up to take their knucklebones from the hollow of the great shield.

'Well, whoever it was that asked,' said Orm, 'what are we three going to answer?'

Only we three, out of the whole crew of the old *Red Witch*; we knew that. Four men we had lost during the summer's fighting, and Hakon One-Eye had already said that if the Emperor *did* form a new bodyguard it would be for young men, and he was too old to change his ways. He was for pushing south and a winter's trading, and those that were left of the crew, and a few others, were throwing in their lot with him; they had their gift-gold to get together a fresh cargo.

Thormod and I looked at each other; but although it was he who had voiced the question, Orm had no doubts. 'There's not like to be too much time of peace, with the Bulgars still loose in Thrace, and if there's rich looting to be had in time of war, that's good enough for me.'

'And there was nothing said as to the laying-by of old blood-feuds,' said a voice behind me.

I swung round, and it was Anders; and his mouth was grave but those odd grey and blue eyes of his were dancing.

'So you're for taking one of the Emperor's knucklebones?' Thormod said—he might have been speaking to another of the *Red Witch*'s crew, save that a muscle twitched at the angle of his jaw.

'It's not likely that we shall ever have another chance to serve in an Emperor's bodyguard, and I'm for trying anything once, to see what it tastes like.'

'Even if it is for only a day, or a few days? The War Host is already disbanded.'

'Is it the things that last only a day that taste the sweetest on the tongue,' Anders said.

And on the surface, they laughed.

I think Orm understood them better than I did. . . .

Well, so the four of us went up and took our knucklebones together from the hollow of the shield before Khan Vladimir's tent. And the oath that three of us had sworn two years since, on Kiev marshes, was blown away like thistledown on the morning wind; and we were free to take up the old Blood Feud again.

We were ordered quite simply—it is all much more complicated now—into ten companies of a hundred, each under our own Illarch, our own Hundred Commander, with Erland Silkbeard over all; and next day at noon, in the great Hippodrome which is used for many kinds of gatherings and public occasions as well as the chariot races for which it was built, we carried our shields before the Emperor for the first time. Oh, Constantine was there too, lounging around the Imperial Box flanked by its huge bronze horses, playing with a hound and laughing behind his hand with a favourite eunuch; but he was too bored to do more than glance at us, and so we did not trouble to give much heed to him. It was to the Emperor Basil, more plainly clad than any of his nobles, and standing in his usual position with his hands on his hips, his moustaches bristling to the noonday sun, that we swore our loyalty, formally setting our drawn swords at his service for life or death. We wore the grey chainmail and nut-shaped helmets that we had worn all summer long; but they had left us our own weapons that we had carried down from the north, murderous pole-axe and light, deadly throwing-axe and the great two-handed Viking sword. All that is changed now also and the Varangians carry the weapons of Byzantium; but that day we saluted the Emperor with our own weapons, and were glad.

And that night, proud as fighting cocks in our new white ceremonial tunics with the thick blocks of embroidery on breast and shoulders, and our cloaks of fine Khazan wool fringed with hanging silver acorns, we stood our first turn of duty as Palace Guards.

The Imperial Palace is like a city in itself, palaces and pleasure pavilions, armouries and stables, even the lighthouse and the Royal Mint, all set in shady gardens sloping to the Bosphorus. And everywhere one looks one sees beauty and strength and splendour. In the greatest things, the mighty tower of the lighthouse with its blazing crest of flame that speaks to shipping far across the waters of

Marmera and up the straits towards the inland sea; in the smallest
—the colonnade before the Emperor's private quarters, opening
on to a tiny court, and in the court a tiny tree whose leaves were
all of beaten gold. Every time I turned in my sentry walk to and
fro, I saw that little tree, its shining leaves touched by the white
light of a waning moon and the red light of the cresset that burned
at the end of the colonnade, and among the leaves, tiny golden
birds that seemed as though in another moment they must break
out singing. So the Emperor could have summer in his little
golden tree, even when there was snow on the ground. A god could
do no more.

And I, who had felt the chafe of a thrall-ring on my neck, felt
now the light pressure of a golden collar. The rest of the Army,
even the guards, do not wear golden collars, only the Varangians;
it is our badge, our own especial honour.

Yet it did not seem to me that night had such a proud shine to
it as the night when the crew of the old *Red Witch* had mounted
guard over the Emperor's tent after Abydos.

15 The Emperor's Hunting

Nex day, the Third Company—that was my Company, and Thormod's and Orm's—Anders' was the Fifth—was ordered across the City to the Blachernae, the small palace tucked away beyond the timber yards and fish quays of the Golden Horn.

The Blachernae is a hunting palace of many stables and kennels, for being close under the land walls it saves having to get the horses and the hounds or cheetahs right across the city every time the Emperor wishes to ride out after boar or gazelle. It is also the place where the Emperors withdraw when they wish to pray at the nearby Church of St. Mary, a great place of pilgrimage by reason of the Virgin's robe, which is its cherished and most sacred possession.

Well, so the Emperor Basil went to pray, and we, the Third Company of his Barbarian Guard, went with him.

That night we had the first of the autumn thunderstorms. It was as though all Miklagard sighed under the rain, stretching and slackening after the long heat. And the next morning the Emperor took a day off from the solid work of ruling his Empire (I have never known any man so strong for sheer hard work, whether it was soldier's work or the duller business of administration), to go hunting with a few of his nobles.

Orders came down to the guardroom, for eight of us to hunt with him. 'It must be hard to be an Emperor and not free even to chase a little gazelle unguarded,' someone said.

Eight of us were ordered out, myself among them, since I was one of the first that the Illarch's eye chanced to fall upon. Orm, who was left on Palace duty along with Thormod, had a few things to say about those who hung around under the eye of their superiors, and so got themselves a day's hunting while their friends had to work.

The eight of us rubbed the sleep out of our eyes—the morning sky was still green beyond the high guardroom windows, and the lamps that burned all night were still casting thick shadows—and pulled on old leather jerkins instead of our fine linen tunics, hurriedly downed some bread and meat and a few swallows of ale, and headed for the palace forecourt, where the horses were being brought out, and the leashed hunting leopards.

The Emperor and his companions came out, and mounted their fretting horses. The huntsmen were up already, with the cheetahs clinging to the pads behind their saddles. Horses used for hunting with leopards are carefully made used to the beasts they carry on their backs; but every horse is born afraid of leopard as they are born afraid of fire; and you could see how they trembled and showed the whites of their eyes when the beasts leapt shadow-light on to their haunches. We of the Guard swung into our saddles. I mind now the quick thrill of pleasure in that moment, for though our mounts were not much taller than ponies, they had Arab blood in them, and I had never had such a fine beast between my knees before. And with the sun scarcely into the sky behind us, we were out through the Palace gates and the Kirkoporta close by, and heading across the churned and littered valley where the Viking camp had lately been, for the low hills westward.

The hills were parched tawny, and the warmth beat up from the ground even while our shadows still ran on eager as hounds before us; but in the dry white watercourses there was dampness under the stones; even a dwindling pool here and there, left by the night's rain; and scent, that had been dried out by the summer's sun, had already begun to return to the world; the faint green scent of grass and oleander leaves, and the aromatic breath of sage and lentisk and rosemary from the hillside scrub.

Scents of another kind, too, that we could not catch, but that made the cheetahs lift their muzzles to the faint breeze, searching the distance with those strange amber eyes. Hunting with cheetah, I soon found, is not at all like hunting with hounds. They are not

pack-hunting animals, and one does not unleash them as a pack
after the quarry, but one or two at a time. They can run faster
than any hound I ever knew; so that their quarry scarcely ever
escapes them. It is for that reason, maybe, that I never really
liked hunting with them. Besides, one cannot think with cheetah
as one can with hounds. . . .

We had good hunting and killed several times. And at last, the
carcasses flung across the backs of the pack ponies and our shadows
growing long once more, we turned back towards Miklagard. But
when the huntsmen came to leash the cheetahs again, one of them
was missing. She would not come for shouting nor for sound of
horn; in all likelihood she was already far beyond hearing. And
while the rest of the hunt followed the Emperor on his homeward
way, a handful of us, mostly huntsmen, scattered to search for
her. Why I was one of them I do not know; maybe, being used to
rounding up strayed cattle, I had some idea tht I had a special
skill for rounding up strayed cheetah. Maybe Fate touched me
on the forehead; I do not know.

What wind there was had gone round with the evening and was
coming from the north. The merest whisper again, but it might
have carried with it some scent of game that had called the creature
to her own hunting; so two or three of us turned northward. Our
ponies were weary, their speed gone from them, and we should
probably be out all night, unless she had killed nearby and we had
the luck to find her on the carcass; but a trained hunting leopard is
a valuable animal, and a deadly one, and not for leaving loose on
a countryside.

We split up, fanning out in our search, and soon I had lost all
touch with the others. I was in autumn-touched birch and bracken
country that reminded me a little of my old world, save that the
mountains of Thrace, blue in the westering distance, were different
from any hills that I had known before, and the sunlight was a
different colour, and the scent of lentisk and wild lavender mingling
with the breath of the bracken was no scent of England. I came
on a track looping down a shallow lightly-wooded valley, and on
the far side, beyond the dusty wayside scrub, a plantation of
almond trees, green and cared for. I must be on the edge of a farm
or one of the small country estates some of the well-to-do have
to provide them with fresh food and summer lodging outside the

city. I checked the pony and sat for a few moments, wondering which way now. I remember now the close evening stillness, and the chirring of the cicadas that was like a voice given to the silence and the heat. And then, from somewhere down the track, where it swung left and was lost behind the almond trees, I heard, almost in the same instant, the terrified cry of something that might be a goat or a deer, and the coughing snarl of a leopard, and a woman's scream.

I drove my heel into the pony's flank, sending him plunging forward. The stones of the track scattered backward under his hooves, and the tangled worry of sounds swelled nearer; at the turn of the track I hauled him back on his haunches and dropped from the saddle. I flung aside the lasso and the lure of meat I carried with me—there would be no time for those—and freed my hunting-knife as I ran, crashing through the scrub towards the yowling of a leopard on its kill. I came out through the aromatic tangle into open beyond the last of the almond trees— and saw what was there to see.

Among the twisted roots of an ancient wild olive, a girl was huddled over something that she was trying to protect from the cheetah, who crouched before her, striking out with taloned paws. I saw the red streaks on her arm and on the fallow hide of the thing she shielded, as I ran in with my knife. I flung myself on the creature as it half-turned on me, got my arm under its chin and drove in the blade. I felt the hot blood spurt over my hand as I heaved the brute aside from the two among the olive roots.

The girl looked up at me, unmoving. Everything was suddenly very silent. I saw the blood welling from three long gashes in her forearm, and turned to the first thing that must be done.

'Your arm—you're bleeding like a pig.' I held out my knife. 'Cut me the hem from your skirt.'

'It can wait. We must help Maia.'

'You first,' I said. 'Will you do it, or shall I?'

She was one—I saw it even in that moment—who would not waste time in useless protesting. She got up, holding out her hand for the dagger, and slashed through the hem of her gown, then ripped off the long blue strip as quickly and without fuss as a man might have done. I took it from her and bound it round her arm;

knotting it off cruelly tight to stop the bleeding. 'That will serve until it can be bathed and properly bandaged.'

She never flinched; but she pulled free and knelt again beside the. gazelle almost before the knot was tied. 'Your hunting has been fine sport.'

'Not mine,' I said, 'the Emperor's.'

'Then I wish him joy of it.'

'The beast ran off on its own.'

'It must have caught the scent,' she said dully, her arms round the gazelle, her cheek down against its dappled hide. 'She never goes so far from the house. She must have strayed off to drop the fawn—and it caught the scent. . . .'

I knelt down also. The gazelle was indeed in labour, and the fawn near to birth; but her beautiful hide was ripped and seamed with crimson at the neck, and the soft eyes already beginning to film over. She lifted her head as her mistress called her name, then let it fall back on to the girl's knee, and a great shudder ran through her.

The girl looked up at me, quite calmly. 'She's dead.'

I nodded. 'I am sorry. But we might save the fawn.' I felt, quickly, but the fawn was not quite near enough to birth for me to get hold of it; and if it was to be saved, there was not a heart beat of time to spare. Once, I had helped old Gyrth to bring a living calf into the world after the mother had died; and I had not known until that moment, that I remembered.

I took up my knife from the grass, still juicily red with the blood of the cheetah. 'Let me have her,' I said, 'and look the other way.' And I lifted the limp carcass from her lap and laid it in the position I wanted.

She made no protest; no sound at all.

Only, again in the evening silence, the cicadas were churring.

I cut, quickly and carefully. I must cut deep and clean, there was no time for fumbling, and yet not deep enough to harm the young one trapped within its dead mother. I laid aside the knife, and put my hands into the hole that I had made. I had the fawn. I pulled it out, deliberately breaking the life-cord as I did so, since among cattle and deer that is the natural way of things. I felt the life stir faintly under my hands; and it was a good feeling. I began to rub away the dark birth-damp with handfuls of summer-dry grass; then went on rubbing with my empty hands, until suddenly the small thing shuddered—but this was a shudder of life coming, not life going—and sneezed, and began to make vague kicking movements with its legs. A she-fawn, and living! I looked at it, already beautiful, the still-damp tawny hide dappled as though with the sun-spots and shadows of the olive leaves. Then I got up and turned round to the girl. She was standing quietly waiting, against the twisted trunk of the old tree; and I knew that from first to last, she had not looked the other way. She held out her arms, and I put the fawn into them.

'I am sorry that I could not save the dam, but here is the daughter for you.'

She looked at the fawn, then up into my face. 'It is a wonderful thing, that you have done this for me,' she said. 'And I think that I must thank you for my own life also.'

There was a stillness about her; I noticed it even then, and thought that not many girls would be so quiet at such a time. And it was in that moment, in the quiet of that moment, that I first really saw her.

She was about my own age, or maybe a year or so younger; her face almond-shaped and almond-coloured, set with long very dark eyes in the paleness of it, and a wide grave mouth. Her dark hair that had been knotted up in an embroidered kerchief, was breaking loose and falling about her shoulders. She wore a straight blue gown, rough as any farm girl's, and splashed and spotted now with blood. But her kerchief had gold threads in its embroidery, and I saw—not by the gold threads alone—that she was no farm girl.

'Where is your house?' I said, glancing about me as though I expected it to spring up among the almond trees. 'There will be time enough for thanks when you are safely home.'

'Are there more leopards loose from the Emperor's hunting, then?' she said. 'Nay, but come you back to the house with me, and wash off the blood while I teach this small one to suck.' She looked down at the little creature in her arms, and then at its dead mother. 'I will send one of the men to look to Maia—and the leopard.'

'I must take the leopard back to its master,' I said.

'So. And there will be trouble?'

'I do not know. But like enough, there will be trouble.'

'Meanwhile, come up to the house.'

So we went up through the almond trees, and skirted a walled olive garth beyond; and so came to the house: not tall and narrow like the houses in the city, but long and low, forming one side of a courtyard, with farm buildings round the other three. In the courtyard an oleander arched over a stone wall-head and a brilliant painted Persian cock strutted among his duller hens. The main room of the house was full of dusk, though there was still an echo of sunlight in the sky outside. A great clattering of pots and pans came from some room beyond. The girl called 'Cloe!' but there was no answer, and the clattering went on unabated.

'She grows deaf,' said the girl, 'and everyone else is out in the lower garden, harvesting the green olives. That is why no one heard me—save you.' She gave the fawn back to me—'Bide here, I'll not be long'—and left me sitting on a cushioned bench just within the door, with the tiny creature on my knees. I heard her from the next room, speaking slowly and clearly to somebody, and the clattering gave place to clucking lamentations. When she came back, she brought a lamp with her, and set it on the table, and the room sprang out of its gathering shadows into a golden glow. It was a room of contrasts, like the girl herself; a floor of beaten earth, but a silk rug, as golden as the lamplight, hanging on one of the rough-plastered walls; and the lamp itself of fine blue-glazed pottery. She looked at me in the new light, and I saw a faint shadow of laughter at the corners of her mouth.

'What is it?' I asked.

'I was wondering what your comrades of the Barbarian Guard would think of you now—though to be sure, you are suitably bloody.'

My mouth must have opened wide enough to catch a cuckoo. 'How did you know?'

'I don't live all my life here on the farm,' she said. 'I saw Khan Vladimir's men roistering through the streets of Constantinople often enough last winter. And old Michael was in the city yester-day with a cartload of farm stuff, and brought back word of the Emperor's new bodyguard. You wear the Imperial Guard's buckle on your belt, and yet your hair is long like a Northman's—and I put all these things together, and guessed.'

A fat old woman shuffled in from the further room, her face crumpled and distressful, a basin and great jug of hot water in her hands. The girl took them from her and set them on the table beside the lamp.

The old woman's gaze was on her roughly bandaged arm. 'Now let me tend to that—tak, tck! I never saw such clumsy binding!'

'Thank you, Cloe dear—no, I can deal with all things here. Now go and send one of the men to fetch Maia as I told you.'

And when the old woman had departed, still clucking and protesting dolefully, the girl fetched strips of fresh linen and a flask of some pungent smelling salve from a chest in the corner.

She brought an old soft rug, too, and made it into a nest on the floor. 'Now, put the fawn down and come here. We must salve our own hurts, or each other's; Cloe means well, but she is too heavy-handed.'

So I did as she bade me, and came to the table; and there in the bright heart of the lamplight, we washed off the blood and cleaned and salved each other's hurts—though mine was the merest scratch, and most of the blood on me was the leopard's—like friends after battle. And looking at the reddened water in the bowl, I thought suddenly of the moon-white night in the apple garth at Sitricstead. . . .

After, when I had finished re-binding the claw slashes on her arm, she brought wine in a cup of green crystal, and while I drank it, gathered up the fawn from its nest, and sat with it on her lap, coaxing it to drink by sucking at her fingers cupped in a bowl of milk. Many's the calf I have taught that way. 'See, baba, suck; the milk is good—so shall you grow strong and beautiful. . . .'

But suddenly there was a tremor in her voice, and something bright fell on the fawn's head. She dashed the back of her hand quickly across her eyes, like a child too proud to let it be seen that she had been crying; and added a smear of milk to make things worse. I set down the wine-cup, and got up. I was glad in a way, for it had seemed to me that she was too quiet and too controlled for her own good; but still, I did not know what to do. 'Is it Maia?' I asked, which was a fool question.

'I had her for more than three years, ever since I found her on the stream bank, abandoned by her mother—and not much bigger than this one—and now . . .'

'I am sorry,' I said. 'I wish there was a thing—anything, that· I could do.'

'You saved the fawn for me. I shall call her Maia, too. And I shall remember always, how you saved her for me.' She looked up. 'What name shall I remember you by?'

'Jestyn,' I said. 'Sometimes Jestyn Englishman.'

I never asked her name, and she did not tell it to me. I touched the fawn's head, still damp where her tears had fallen on it. 'May the small one flourish,' I said.

And I went out into the twilit courtyard, leaving her sitting in the pool of lamplight, with her head bent over the tiny creature in her lap. I went back through the almond trees, wondering if I should have to spend half the night trailing my horse. But a hunting-pony is trained in such things, and he had wandered only a little way, and came to my whistle. I gathered up the body of the cheetah from where it still lay under the wild olive tree, and flung it across his withers. The farm people had fetched away the dead gazelle, and the next rain would wash the blood from the grass.

Then I mounted the pony and headed back for Miklagard.

Later that night there was a certain amount of unpleasantness, when I confronted the Master of the Hunting Kennels, with the cheetah's body lying on the ground between us.

'There was no time to swither around with the lure and the lasso. I had to kill her to save the girl,' I told him, after I had heard him out. 'If your huntsmen were better at their work—'

His eyes narrowed. 'Well, like enough, you'll soon be back to your own kind of work—your own kind of hunting.'

'Meaning?'

'Haven't you heard the rumour? It was around all day.'

'I came straight to bring you this—' I stirred the cheetah's body with my foot. 'I've had no word with anyone on the way.'

'They're saying that your fine new Barbarian Guard—two or three Companies of you at any rate—are being sent off to join John of Chaldea in Thrace. Bulgar hunting.'

16 'He still had his gold collar on'

I reported back to the Illarch—Thrand Ericson, that was, but mostly, from his seafaring days, he went by the name of Thrand Thunderfist from the way he had of showing when he was not pleased with any of his crew. Himself, he was one of the biggest men I have ever known. I reported back, and went off to join the rest.

The Guardroom was hazy with lamp-smoke; and men were sitting on the benches or lounging around the open doorway to the Armourer's Court, playing Fox-and-Geese or cleaning their gear. One man was sitting on the floor with his bare feet stuck straight out before him, playing an alder pipe and wagging time to the tune with his big toes. I looked around for Thormod, but could not see him, nor Orm, for that matter.

Then Gunna Butason looked up from his game and saw me. 'Aha, Jestyn is back to the fold. Did you find the cheetah?'

'Yes,' I said. 'I found the cheetah. Where's Thormod?'

'Gone off with Orm and a few more. Our company wasn't good enough for them, so they went seeking for better.'

'Where?' I said.

Gunna shrugged his shoulders; but Wulf Aikinson spat on the belt buckle he was polishing and said, 'The Silver Salamanda, I'd not wonder.'

'Have you heard the rumour?' somebody put in.

'Yes, I've heard.' There was a sudden uneasiness at the back of my mind. The Silver Salamanda had been a favourite meeting-place from the first, for the Viking Kind. It was about midway between the Blachernac and the Imperial Palace; and with word going round that in a few days the Varangian Guard would be split up and some of us sent to Thrace, it seemed horribly likely that Thormod and Anders would be heading that way, looking for each other.

'I'll go after them,' I said.

'Best go across to the kitchen and get a bite in your belly first.'

'I'm not hungry,' I said, and flung round and headed back through the outer Court to the Night Gate. The main gates of both the Blachernae and the Imperial Palace were closed at three o'clock every afternoon until the following dawn, as a sign that for that day official business of state was over, and for the rest of the day the lives of the Emperor and his Court were their own. After that, all going and coming was by one of the side gates. I was afraid I might have trouble getting out, so late in the night. But I knew some of the Gate Guard; and from the first, the Varangians have been pretty much a law unto themselves. So beyond a few jeering inquiries as to whether my mother knew I was abroad at that hour (I was still young-looking for my nineteen years, my beard no more than a yellow fuzz), I got through without trouble and set out for the Silver Salamanda.

It was very late when I got there; but the long low-ceilinged room was still crowded, loud with voices and thick with lamp smitch and the smell of wine and sweat and the meat roasting over charcoal braziers at the far end. Again I could see no sign of Thormod; but a handful of our lads were gathered in a corner playing dice, and among them I could make out Orm's big sandy head. I pushed my way across the room towards him, dodging elbows and stepping over sprawling legs.

He looked up and saw me coming, and checked between throw and throw.

'Where's Thormod?' I said.

'You're late back from your hunting.'

'One of the cheetahs went missing. Where's Thormod?'

'Gone with Anders Herulfson,' he said, and made his throw.

I heard the rattle of the dice as though in a sudden silence. Neither of us looked to see what he had thrown.

'Just—the two of them?'

He nodded. 'He came looking for Anders, and in a while Anders came looking for him. They drank together, and then they went out.'

'And you let him go, and stayed here, playing dice?'

He quirked up his sandy brows above those lazy grey-green eyes. 'It's not my feud.'

'No,' I said. 'It's mine.'

And I turned and made for the door.

'They went downhill,' somebody shouted after me.

So I headed downhill towards the sea walls, and the quaysides along the Golden Horn. There would be few people along the waterfront at that hour. Space to finish a Holm Ganging that had begun on Kiev marshes, two years ago. . . .

In the dim streets, the torches burning at corners cast pools of fish-scale light across the cobbles, with long secret stretches of shadow between, and there were other, moving shadows, of people, and voices that seemed shadowy also, and sometimes a snatch of laughter. And I remembered suddenly and sharply another night when I had hunted Thormod through the winding ways of Dublin, with his piece of amber stowed in the breast of my sark, and something of the same fear upon me that was cold upon me now.

Somewhere in the distance I could hear a hubbub which was like enough a band of Varangians—the city was full of our kind that night, raising a triumphal uproar in praise of the Emperor's new bodyguard.

It grew fainter behind me as I passed out by the gate on to the lower Fish Quay. A little movement of air came to meet me off the water. There was the faint cool snail-shine of a low moon, and the night was pinpricked by lights from the houses of Sycae across the Horn. I heard the slapping of the dark water among the boats below the quay, and far off, the rumble of cartwheels, the bark of a dog, all the ordinary sounds of Miklagard by night. I rounded a pile of masts and rigging and a couple of sails spread out to dry— and saw Thormod. Just Thormod, standing with his back to me, where the light of a cresset on the corner of a warehouse wall spilled over the edge of the quay into the water. He was looking down, and he barely glanced round as I went towards him, knowing my step, I suppose then looked down again. I also. It was wolf-black among the boats under the wall, and nothing moved but the water tonguing at the mooring-posts. Of Anders, no sign at all.

'My knife took him under the ribs,' Thormod said, in that dead-level voice of his. 'He must have been fish-bait before he hit the water.'

I nodded. The weight of his high studded boots and sword-belt and the gold collar about his neck would have been enough between them to carry his body straight down. 'So it is finished,' I said, with relief that was like the sudden ending of physical pain.

But there was a kind of grief in me, all the same.

'He slipped on a bit of stinking fish,' Thormod said.

And then, with a dark swirl of movement and voices upraised in singing, a bunch of the Varangians in full cry came spilling out from a side alley on to the end of the quay. You could know them even at that distance and in the dark, for they were yelling a faintly recognizable version of one of the rowing lilts that I had come to know during the long days on shipboard; and even drunk, no one but a Northman could make that hellish din.

Thormod looked at the dagger in his hand. In the cresset light it showed reddened to the hilt. But he had nothing to clean it on except his tunic or breeks, where the stain would show up like a wolf's kill on a snowfield. He thrust it back into its sheath to wait for cleaning later; and we turned away from the quay, back towards the sea walls.

The Blood Feud was over and done with, no good purpose would be served by getting the rest of the Varangians tangled in the web of it.

By noon next day, word had found its way across the City from the Imperial Palace, and as we sat at our midday pork and greens in the Blachernae mess hall, suddenly I caught the name through the surf of voices: 'Anders Herulfson—Anders Herulfson. . . .'

Anders Herulfson had been found at dawn, by some fishermen going to take out their boats, hanging on to a mooring rope, with a stab wound under his ribs, and was now in the Garrison hospital. 'Who did it?' someone at our table asked, craning backwards for the answer.

And somebody checked in passing. 'Set on by robbers, so he said—too dark to see their faces, so he'd not remember them again. The odd thing is that he still had his gold collar on.'

'Maybe they were disturbed before they could get it off him.'

'How bad is the wound?'

'He'll likely live.'

'Then I'd say the hole in his hide must be less than the hole in his memory,' said Orm, sitting across the table from me. His eyes met mine, and there was a quirk to his sandy eyebrows.

Beside me, Thormod, his mouth full of poppyseed bread, put up a hand and idly pulled at his sleeve, making sure that it had not ridden up to show a blood-stained rag knotted above his elbow.

I did nothing; neither moved nor spoke nor even thought, just sat there feeling rather as though someone had kneed me in the belly.

It was evening before Thormod and I could speak alone together. We were off-duty then, and taking our ease by the cistern of Theodosius, which is a pleasant place, with shady trees about the arched entrance, and grass to sit on, and a coolness that seems to breathe up from the hidden water. I was sitting with my back against the patchy trunk of a plane tree, Thormod lying beside me, his head on his arms staring up into the branches. Women passed and re-passed with their great jars empty or dripping with the evening water.

'And now?' I said, when we had been silent a long while with the same thing in both our minds.

'We must wait, yet again,' Thormod said.

'It is in my mind that already there has been overmuch of waiting.'

Thormod turned his head on his arms; he might have been talking over the price of radishes. 'Men have waited longer than this, for the clearing of a blood debt.' And then with a sudden change of mood, he rolled over and banged his fist on the turf. 'If I had thought for an instant that there was yet a spark of life in him, I would have gone down and finished him as a hunter finishes a wounded animal. Now. . . .'

'They'll not keep much of a guard on the sick quarters,' I said. He looked at me. 'Could you do that?'

'I don't know. It is not my feud.' The thing was said before I knew it, and I could not take it back.

There was a sharp moment of silence; and then he said, 'No, it is not your feud—in spite of this. . . .' And he reached out and touched the little white scar inside my wrist.

I turned my hand over quickly and touched the matching scar on his. 'It *is* mine, because it is yours, but—still I do not know.'

He smiled lazily. 'We'll not argue the thing. It is my feud, I know. I could have finished him like a wounded beast, last night. Now, the moment is past and cold, and I can only wait. If he dies, I shall have killed him anyway; and if he lives—I must wait until he can give me a fight.'

'And if he never can? A knife-wound under the ribs is apt to leave havoc behind it.'

'If he lives, yet does not win back to his fighting strength, then I shall know that there is no justice in my own gods. Maybe I will even turn to your White Kristni.'

17 Death in Thrace

The rumour that we were being sent to Thrace turned out to be true; and a few days later, changed back from our gold-embroidered tunics into battle-grey mail, we were on the march. At this end of the world, where the winters are not so cold, War Hosts do not break off their wars during the dark months of the year, as they do in the north. Indeed, so far as cavalry is concerned, there is better grazing for the horses in the winter than in the hot months when the sun has burned the open hillsides brown. I remember cold winter nights, for all that, sleet blowing in the wind; watch-fires in the mountains, when we slept huddled close for warmth with our cloaks about us and our feet to the flames; skirmishes fought out in the teeth of a wind that cut like a flaying knife; wolves howling uncomfortably close about the horse lines.

Through that winter we were for the most part on our own. A Bandon of cavalry, a few Centuries of regular troops, and us—three companies of the Emperor's new Barbarian Guard, out to prove ourselves the best, at least the most terrible, fighting men in the Empire.

We had no big-scale fighting in those months, but a fair deal of skirmishing, for our task was to hold and harry the Bulgars and the Khazan tribesmen from the north, until with the spring, Basil should bring up more troops to thrust them westward. We did not know that we were beginning the Emperor's life's work for him: the driving back of the Bulgarian frontier to what it was in Justinian's day, bringing all the lands between Macedonia and the Danube, the Inland Sea and the Adriatic again into the Byzantine Empire. It is done now. Thirty years in the doing, and treaties made and treaties broken, and a whole captured Bulgarian Army blinded along the way. (The Emperor Basil is nothing if not thorough!) But the priests tell us that it is God's Will. And God's Will is done.

But that winter, with no knowledge of any such great over-all plan, with no news from the city, we followed John of Chaldea, that white-faced, black-bearded man with a fire in his belly, in a kind of small ragged war of our own. Once, towards winter's end, a supply train got through to us, with dispatches for the Commander, and news that got loose and ran from camp fire to camp fire in a gale of laughter.

Basil, it seemed, had listened to the tears and pleading of his sister the Princess Anna, and tried to back out of his bargain with Khan Vladimir. But at the first hint of delay about sending him his promised bride, Vladimir had seized the Byzantine port of Cherson on the Inland Sea, and threatened to do the same to Miklagard itself. 'So our Basil has had to give in, and hand the lady over, for all her tears,' said one of the supply-wagon men, sitting at our fire.

I laughed with the rest, but I was still sorry for the Princess Anna. Ah well, if what I hear be true, she has had none so ill a life of it. At least she has borne sons who are like to be emperors themselves one day, and that should count for something with an Emperor's sister. If I am sorry for her even now, it must be that I am a foolish old man.

'The Emperor must be of a meeker temper than I had thought,' said Orm, through a mouthful of wild pig.

'Why, as to that,' one of the escort riders who had also joined us, leaned forward and helped himself to the wine jar, 'he's about as meek as a mountain bear, but he's got more sense. He knows he's got few enough troops to take on the Bulgars and the Khazan hoards *and* Khan Vladimir at the same time, and even some of the troops he has—'

The man checked, and Orm said blandly, 'What of the troops he has, friend?'

'Do you think he can be sure yet, of his new Barbarian Guard?' the other said, grinning.

I thought there was going to be a fight after that. Maybe it was only because we were all so tired, and had had a winter's fighting anyway, that there was not. But I mind, even after we had got things sorted out, Thormod with his head high on his shoulders, and his brows almost meeting above the root of his nose, demanding, 'Does he not understand, this Emperor of ours, who seeks to duck out from under his own promises, that when the Northmen sell their swords, they keep their share of the bargain?'

'Even against their own kind?' said the escortman.

'They keep their share of the bargain,' Thormod said again, levelly.

'So long as the man who buys, keeps his,' Orm added. 'If he doesn't, then we put the swords to another use.' And he drew his finger across his throat. 'But clearly our little Basil is a man who keeps his bargains, even if sometimes a shade unwillingly. So—our service is his so long as he pays for it, and we die for him if need be. Quite a few of us have already; he needn't lie awake at night under his gold and purple coverlid, worrying about that.'

Spring came, with an outburst of sudden small flame-bright flowers that were not the flowers of an English spring, and lacking something of the birdsong. And with the spring, the Emperor came up with the long awaited troops. I mind the day he rode in, the camp resounding to shouted orders and trumpet calls and the whinnying and trampling of horses; the Emperor's great blue and purple pavilion going up, and almost before the last rope was made fast, the Varangians mounting guard around it. Three Companies of the Varangians had come up with him, to relieve us, the three who had been up there all winter long and would be marching eastward in a few days, to take over Palace duty guarding the Emperor Constantine.

That evening, as the shadows began to lengthen, the camp was full of reunions, as men strolled to and fro in search of old friends and comrades—or old enemies. I was kicking my heels among the crowd that had gathered about the Field Armoury, waiting to have a dint knocked out of my shield boss. The Armoury, with its red roar of flame from the forge fire, and the cheerful ding of hammer on anvil, is always a favourite gathering-place in any camp, whether or not one has need of the armourer's skill, and some of the crowd had nothing for mending at all, but had merely drifted that way as one might to a wine-shop. Orm and Thormod were there too; and a small knot of newcomers, some of them still eating the remains of their evening meal, wandered up to join us—Varangians from the Palace Guard, whose place we should soon be taking.

And one of them, with a great collop of pigmeat in his hand, was Anders Herulfson.

Anders Herulfson, living or dead. For a moment, seeing him between the fading daylight and the red glow of the forge fire, I was not sure which, and the hairs crept on the back of my neck.

Then somebody let out a shout: 'Well! See who's here among us! Anders Herulfson!'

'Or his ghost,' somebody else said. 'Man! When they fished you out of the Horn that morning, I'd not have wagered much on the likelihood of seeing you carrying your sword again, this side the Rainbow Bridge!'

'And you as good as new, and eating hearty,' Orm added.

Anders spat out a piece of gristle, and grinned briefly. 'As good as new,' he agreed, 'save when something still catches me under the ribs—like a bee-sting, when I laugh. Just enough to keep me from forgetting how I came to be in the Horn that morning. No more.'

I don't think he and Thormod even looked at each other.

The smith was shouting at me. 'Hi! You! Do you want that dint beaten out or not?'

And when I had handed over my shield, and looked round again, Anders was gone. 'Where is he?' I asked, stupidly.

Thormod looked round at me slowly, the corners curling a little on that straight mouth of his. 'Gone about his own affairs for now. But I'm thinking I'll not need to turn from my own gods to your White Kristni just yet, after all.'

Two days later, we drove the Bulgars out of a small strong hill-town they had held all winter. We attacked at first light. It had been raining in the night, and I remember the smell of morning on the grass as we went in to the attack.

The Bulgars were ready for us, and it was hot work for a while, among the half-ruined walls of the town, and through the narrow ways whose own people had been killed or driven out months

before. Orm was killed in the first rush; we weren't doing too
badly at keeping our part of the Emperor's bargain. He gave a
surprised grunt and dropped just ahead of me with a Bulgar spear
in his belly. The man put his foot on Orm's body to drag the
spearhead out—his breeks were striped red and white and blue,
so he must have been a noble. It's odd, the things one notices
sometimes—I got him in that moment, my sword under his arm;
but I didn't have time for feeling anything, as I thrust on after
the great sweeping war-axe of Thrand Thunderfist. There would
be time for feeling, later.

We made a fine killing, and by noon the streets and alleyways
were blood-spattered, piled with dead in the gateways and at
corners where the fighting had been most fierce, with the smell of
the knacker's yard about them; and we were hunting fugitives
through the hillside scrub.

Left to ourselves, I doubt if the Varangians would have hunted
that trail, for the Viking Kind do not care much about fugitives,
unless they have a score to settle. But the Emperor Basil has always
been one for a thorough job, and no loose ends left hanging; and
we had our orders.

Such a hunting can be as dangerous for the hunters as for the
hunted, especially when the hunted are in their own countryside;
for often the hunters may become as widely scattered as their
quarry. . . . So it was that late in the day, into the time of Long
Shadows, Thormod and I and a handful more, found ourselves
in the mouth of a narrow valley, where a little rocky stream came
down from the mountains. A stream that would dry out to bare
bones in the summer; what we call in England a winter bourne,
as are many of the watercourses in those parts. We were tired
and thirsty, three of us were wounded and we stopped to drink
out of our war-caps and bathe our hurts.

When I am tired or anxious, or when the old wound pains me,
I see that little valley in my dreams even now: in a soft clear light
that is not quite the light of this world. Ragged outcrops of the
mountain rock thrusting through the ragged cloak of scrub; an
ancient wild almond in the loop of the watercourse, three parts
dead, yet with one unvanquished branch breaking into a starry
cloud of pale blossom; a peregrine falcon hanging high overhead.
The water was greenish with melting snows far up in the

mountains: ice cold—cold enough to drown the taste of the sweaty leather and the iron rim. Thormod and I drank in turn, both from the same war-cap—mine—and I remember how good the water tasted.

I remember also, how, as Thormod bent to scoop it up, the piece of amber on its thong, swung forward through the slackened-off neck of his mail shirt.

'We'll not find any more now,' Eric Longshanks said, cleaning the blade of his throwing-axe by chopping it into the turf.

And at the same instant, even before Thormod could thrust the amber back inside his mail, Swain let out a shout: 'Look! Up there!'

We looked where he pointed, and something moved, high above us among the birch scrub and hill juniper. Just an instant's flicker of movement, and then for a long moment, nothing more. And then the thing broke cover: a man, running lopsided like a bird with a broken wing, across the bare rock slope before he disappeared into the next patch of scrub. Someone raised the shout of the hunter who views the quarry, and we broke forward after him, scrambling up through the lentisk and juniper.

Once or twice we glimpsed the man ahead of us. He was heading up valley, but seemed to have turned downhill again, making for the thicker cover of the lower slopes and the streamside. We should have been able to outrun him, wounded as he looked to be; but we were leg-weary and there were the three of us who had taken scathe of our own in the fighting; and it was as much as we could do to gain on him at all. Among the hill scrub, running hard, we scarcely noticed how the valley was changing, narrowing in on us, until we came out into the open again, and found ourselves in a rocky defile with the hillsides rising almost shear on either hand. Not a good place to be, in enemy territory. But the man was close in front of us now; one last burst, and we should have him.

I don't know what made me look back as I ran. I saw a flicker of movement in the scrub behind us, the glint of late sunlight on metal.

'Look out!' I yelled. 'They're behind us!'

Almost in the same instant, a flight of stones came whistling down the hillside into our midst. One caught Eric Longshanks on the point of the shoulder and sent him reeling. One caught Swain on the head, and he dropped like a poled ox. Whether he was outright dead, I'd not be knowing; I never saw him again.

I have often wondered how many Bulgars there were; probably not many, but there were no more than seven or eight of us, and save for that flicker among the scrub, we could not see them; we only knew that we were all at once beset on every side; and those accursed stones whistling down on us. We had to stop them at all costs. I mind we started to scramble up the hillside to try to come to grips with our unseen enemy; but it wasn't just pebbles they were throwing, it was sizeable chunks of rock. To keep together was to huddle like sheep for slaughter, and we scattered as we ran. All the hillside seemed coming down on us now. I saw a jagged boulder flying down towards me, and tried to leap clear—and did not quite make it. It took me on my right knee. It did not even hurt, in those first moments; there was just a numbing sense of shock, and I was lying sprawled out with my face in a patch of rough grass. I struggled to get up, but I seemed pinned to the ground by an enormous dragging weight where my right leg ought to be; and when I managed to get on to my elbow, and looked down, my knee had turned into a kind of soggy red mush with splinters of bone sticking out of it.

Somebody was scrambling towards me along the open hillside —Thormod, bending over me, hauling me up into the slim shelter of a rocky outcrop. I glimpsed Bulgar helmets and heard the first ragged shouting of close-fighting begin. 'My knife,' I croaked. 'Give me my knife and get after the rest.'

'We're all going to Valhalla, anyway,' he said. 'You and I will stick together on the road.' And he side-strode over me, sword in hand. For a moment the Thracian hillside darkened and swam, and became a night-time Dublin alleyway; and I heard him, standing tree tall above me, raise the great Viking shout.

Then the hillside swam clear again, and I saw a figure a couple of spear-throws away, sharp-edged in the evening light, that I thought for an instant was one of us, because it wore Varangian harness; and yet it did not carry itself like a friend. . . .

I saw that it was Anders Herulfson, with his light throwing-axe in his hand.

In the last moments before the Bulgars closed in, he came

running lightly between the rocks and the grey hillside scrub, and I saw the circling flash of the axe blade he whirled above his head, the bright, spinning arc of it as he sent it free.

A throwing-axe always seems to be travelling so slowly that there should be time to avoid it. But in truth, there is not.

It took Thormod between the neck and shoulder.

He made a horrible choking sound, cut off short. The blood came in a hot red stinking wave, bursting out over both of us as he crumpled slowly to his knees and then on to his face on top of me, the axe blade still wedged in the bones of his neck. Beyond him I saw Anders almost upon us; his face looking down, somehow not real, like a mask of Anders' face with something piteous and horrible behind it. My turn next. I heaved my right arm free from Thormod's body, struggling to come at my dagger—and on that instant, clear on the evening air, came the silver crowing of Byzantine trumpets.

Anders checked, and for an instant, across Thormod's body, our eyes met. Then he turned and melted into the hillside scrub. There was quick quiet movement all around, as the men who had ambushed us pulled back from the fight. And I wondered, in a detached sort of way, whether he would get clear, from both our own troops and the Bulgars. It seemed heavy odds against.

There was blood everywhere. Thormod's blood and mine, soaking into the ground together, like those few scattered drops on the edge of the apple-garth at Sitricstead; but more of it now— much more. . . .

I was aware of a flurry of men like a flurry of shadows, and the clash of weapons and a cry cut off short, and the squeal of a horse somewhere on the lower slopes that all seemed to be the shadows of sounds far off. Everything was far off, and going further; confused like a sick man's dream. Then the dream cleared a little; and the daylight was fading, and somebody in a cavalry helmet was bending over me, head and shoulders dark against a green crystal sky. Thormod's dead weight was being lifted off me; and someone said, 'Christ! A Viking throwing axe! This was done by one of their own lot!'

And the man bending over me said, 'That can be cleared up later, here's another, with the life still in him.'

And then the buzzing darkness closed over me.

18 Wind Smelling of Wet Grass

So Thormod went to Valhalla alone—no, not alone; he went in good company, but without me. It did not come to me until long after, that that must have been the way of it in any case, for if I had died that day on the Thracian hillside, I would have had another road that I must follow—unless, indeed, I had lost that road for ever when I took my oath with the rest of the old *Red Witch*'s crew on Thor's Ring at Kiev.

Somewhere in the Scriptures, the Christ is set down as saying that in His Father's House there are many mansions; and from that saying, I draw hope that there is a Valhalla for Thormod at the end of the Rainbow Bridge. He and Orm and Hakon One-eye and the rest, they would not be happy in our Christian Heaven; and yet God made them, and I cannot believe in a God who would waste such man-stuff on Damnation. The priests would say that such a thought was sin and heresy. And so I have never spoken it to a priest. I can only trust in God, His mercy.

But as I say, that thinking came later. Much later.

For many days all things were hazy, and my memories of the hospital tents at Berea are as ragged as an old cloak and full of holes, in part, I think, from the effect of the poppy draughts they gave me to deaden the pain of my smashed knee. It is said that a hurt to the knee or elbow or the palm of the hand gives more pain than a hurt of the same size to any other part of the body; a saying which I have remembered since, in my own dealings with injured men.

And my next clear memory is of a sky fiercely blue above me, and the jolting of the ox-cart carrying wounded men back to Constantinople.

I lay staring back at that fierce blue stare of the sky that was like the somehow accusing gaze of the Christ Pantocrator in the roof of the church of St. Irene, and nerving myself to every lurch and judder of the ox-cart under me. The flies were a torment, and I mind fumbling up my hand to brush away one that was stinging my neck, and feeling as I did so, the piece of amber shaped like Thor's Hammer that was stowed inside my tattered sark. The axe-blade that had killed Thormod must have severed the thong, and it had been in my hand when they found me; and someone thinking that it was mine, had knotted the blood-stained thong round my neck. It was warm and alive as though with Thormod's life under my hand, as it is now when I feel for it inside my tunic where it hangs still. It had come to me as a parting gift, a parting command from my blood-brother. And holding it, as the ox-cart jolted onward, I felt the old Blood Feud as my own at last; the feud that had never been quite my own before. Now that it was too late, and somebody else must have killed Anders long ago— Anders, who should have been for my killing, because he had killed Thormod.

And I had lost my brother, and I had lost my enemy, and I had lost my way. . . .

I took the wound fever, and was like to die after all, and so find the way out of all my problems. And for long after the fever let me go, the wound festered and would not heal. And then that passed also. But it was the edge of autumn again before they had done with me in the old military hospital in the heart of the city, and I was free to go where I chose and do what I would, except return to my comrades. No room in the Varangian Guard for a man with a smashed knee, who must swing one leg stiff as a broomstick to the end of his days.

Byzantium plays fair by its soldiers, with a lump sum in good solid gold after their service years are ended. But for the Mercenary, all the world over, it is another thing. We hire out our swords to a Lord who is not our own by birth; we fight for him, and he pays us, and the loot is good, and that is the bargain. But when, through age or wounds, our swords cease to be worth the hiring, the payment stops, and we may find other work if we can, or get ourselves home to wherever we came from, turn beggar or bandit, or drown ourselves in the nearest horse-pond. That is all in the bargain, and fair enough, too, in its way. But with only twenty summers under his belt, a man is something young to find himself on the garbage heap.

The Vargangians would stand by their own in a casual way, I knew, always good for the price of a meal or a drink, maybe even for odd jobs around the barracks. But I had no stomach for hanging around other men's camp fires.

So what should I do now? What road was I to follow?

I remember standing in the narrow crowded street, leaning on my staff—for my knee was barely up to my weight as yet—and wondering what I should do from that moment forward, with the unlived part of my life, long or short, that lay ahead of me. The slow fire that I had lacked and longed for, was burning in my belly now, and the only thing that seemed to me worth doing was to hunt down and kill Anders Herulfson, if by any wild chance he was not dead already. But I had enough sense left to know that, even with a sound knee, to go hunting a man who had almost certainly been dead for months, through the enemy mountains of Thrace would be to run mad. If he lived, he would have a far better chance of finding me; and I knew that I could trust him to come seeking. . . . Dark Thorn had said that I had the mark of the Blood Feud on my forehead. . . .

What in God's name should I do?

I realized suddenly that I was standing almost in the doorway of a little church. And—maybe it was in part to get away from the crowds, for after the months within the long halls and cloistered courts of the old hospital, the constant swirling come and go of the open city made my head swim—I did a thing that I have done all too seldom in my life; I went inside to ask my way.

It was cool and full of shadows inside; faintly smelling of stale incense and candlewax and the coldness of old stone. There was a shimmer of candles before a picture of a woman's face—just the face, dark and almond-shaped, with full dark eyes and a grave mouth, and all the rest of the picture covered with smoky silver. I knew that it was a picture of Christ's Mother, but she reminded me of someone else. I could not think who. I suppose I prayed, though I did not think of it as praying at the time, standing before her, my hands clasped on my staff.

I said, 'Lady, once, for a friend's sake, I took an oath to Thor in a God-House of the Northmen in Kiev, and it may be that for that, I am damned. But if I am not damned, let you ask your Son for me, that He will show me what I must do when I go out from here; for I do not know. I do not know at all.'

I did not even add a candle to those glimmering before the picture, though I had the price of one; the remains of my last pay. But in a while, I turned and went back into the street.

After the shadows and the cold incense smell and the quiet within the church, the sights and sounds and smells of the outside world fell on me like a shout. A sudden gust of wind, warm with the last lingerings of summer, came up the street, raising a little dust cloud and scattering a waft of mingled scents from an unseen garden behind the high wall that joined the church. Somebody must have been watering the grass, for it was the green scent of rain on parched earth and the leaves of trees. And all at once I was filled with an aching longing for open country; and memory flung up in my mind the day almost a year ago, when I had followed the Emperor in his hunting, and the smell of the world after the autumn rain—and I knew who it was that the smoke-darkened face set in dim silver had reminded me of. The girl of the wild olive tree, the girl with the tame gazelle. Standing there in the crowded and noisy street, I remembered her quietness, a cool quietness like shade on a dusty road. . . .

She had brought milk for the fawn; so maybe they had cattle on the farm. If not, I could learn to tend goats. Maybe they needed a goat-herd—or someone to do odd jobs and help with the olive harvest. . . .

And so, for the second time in my life, the wind set me on the road I was to follow.

19 The House of the Physician

I bought bread and black figs at a market stall, and added them to my few possessions bundled in a cloak, and set out.

I went out through the Kirkoporta, the small gate close beside the Blachernae Palace, my shadow already beginning to lengthen behind me, and headed westward into the rolling country. It had not seemed far, that evening coming the other way, with the dead cheetah lying across my horse's withers, but it was a long way now, on foot; and I spent the night on the road, in the corner of a disused cattle fold; and it was not far short of noon next day when I came to the place where the track branched below the farm. I took the right-hand fork, then came up through the almond trees, past the walled olive garden. In the heat of the day, no one seemed to be about, save for an old man snoring in the shade, and the cicadas loud as always among the olive trees.

Fat Cloe came from one of the outbuildings as I reached the farm courtyard, shooing before her a flurry of hens that had evidently got somewhere they should not have been. She gave them a final shoo and abandoned them at sight of me; and standing hands on hips, demanded my business. She did not recognize me. I had not thought she would.

'I came to speak with the lady,' I said.

'Eh? Speak up, whoever you are—everybody mumbles these days.'

I remembered that Cloe was deaf, and asked again more loudly, for the mistress, the one with the fawn.

'There's no need to shout!' said the fat woman. 'If people don't mumble, they shout! It will be the Lady Alexia you're meaning?'

I nodded. I did not know her name, but I knew it must be the Lady Alexia I was meaning.

'She's not here,' said the woman. 'She's in the city.'

'I've just come from there. . . .'

'So you've had a long walk for nothing.' And then I suppose she saw that I was tired and wayworn, and maybe I looked as lost as I suddenly felt; and her face grew kinder. 'Aye, and on that leg—too long a walk, by the looks of you. Sit down in the shade and cool your throat for a start.'

There was a bench under the oleander, and I sat down thankfully, stretching my aching leg out in front of me; and she brought me ice-cold water in an earthen cup, and I drank, and gave the cup back to her. 'I thought she would be here—it's still hot weather—'

She sat down also, and returned to the basket of almonds she must have been shelling when the hens interrupted her. 'Oh no.' She cracked an almond with a stone, and began breaking off the brown shards of husk. 'Even in the summer she's to and fro between here and the city.'

'And she's there now?' I said, stupidly.

'Aye, with her father. He cannot spare her for long; and himself, he seldom has time to come out here at all. So many sick folk there are in the City; and no finer doctor, they tell me, than Alexius Demetriades, in all Constantinople.' She checked, and looked up from her task. 'It was not really him you wanted, for that leg of yours?'

I shook my head. 'I doubt there's any more to be done about that. I came because I thought—I hoped the Lady Alexia might need some work doing—I needed work, and I remembered her—and this place.' I sounded confused in my own ears, but I was so tired.

She let out a screech like a pea-hen. 'Husband!' and a little man as lean and sharp-angled as a cicada appeared, yawning, from another doorway, and grunted inquiringly.

Cloe jerked her head in my direction. 'He's come looking for the Lady Alexia—wants work.'

The little man looked me up and down, and I got wearily to my feet to be looked at. It seemed the best thing to do.

'I'm good with livestock,' I said, 'and I can turn my hand to most things about a farm.'

He pulled at his scraggy beard. 'Does the Lady Alexia know you?'

'She only saw me once, and it was almost a year ago; but I think she would remember me. One of the Emperor's cheetahs ran wild after a day's hunting, and—'

'And some hairy-heeled Viking of the Emperor's new Barbarian Guard saved her when she was attacked by it.'

'It was the gazelle that it was really attacking,' I said.

Cloe let out a squeal. 'He could be the one! Now I come to look at him, he could so!' I have noticed the same thing about some other deaf people, that they can hear none so ill when they want to.

There was a small silence, while the old man took another stare at me. 'Are you telling me you're one of the Barbarian Guard? You don't look like it.'

'Not now,' I said. 'I did—I was, until I got this knee fighting in Thrace in the spring.'

He considered, still tugging at his beard. 'Easy enough to come here with an old soldier's hard-luck story—'

'Don't you believe me, then?'

He sniffed. 'I wouldn't say I don't, and I wouldn't say I do. Either way it makes no odds; I've two men under me, and I can manage with that—just about. I won't say I couldn't do with another hand, but I'm not my own master, to take on extra men without the word of the Lady Alexia or her father.'

'I'm sorry I woke you from your noon sleep for nothing. I'll go.'

'Not so fast,' he said. 'You want the Lady Alexia—you go back to the city and speak with her, and bring me back a bit of parchment with her name writ on it by herself. I can't read, but I know how the Lady Alexia writes her name—and I'll find you work on the farm—so that you do it properly.'

'How shall I find the Lady Alexia in the city?'

'The Street of the Golden Mulberry Tree, close by the Hippodrome. It's the last house on the right-hand side, going up. But anyone round that way will tell you, if you ask for the House of the Physician.'

'I'll be on my way,' I said.

'You do that.'

Cloe cut in, picking up her basket of almonds and lumbering to her feet. 'But not before you've some food in your belly and a night's sleep behind you. For shame, Michael, we don't need the mistress's word to give a night's shelter to a guest.'

She was kind, fat Cloe. She fed me and gave me some broken harness to mend, and an old rug in a corner under the vine arbour for my night's sleep. And in the morning she gave me bread and olives and a draught of thin wine to see me on my way, and said, 'Do not you be cast down. If your story is true, and I'm minded that it is, the more I look at you, the Lady Alexia will remember and be grateful, and her father will help you. They are not folk to let a debt go unpaid.'

She meant it so kindly. Only I had not thought of it like that—not as claiming gratitude and the payment of a debt. It had been only that the wind had smelt of rain on parched grass, and the dark quiet face of the Madonna had brought the girl with the fawn back into my mind, and with it the idea that she might have work for me on the farm—the kind of work that my hands and heart knew. Cloe's kindly meant words took me like a blow in the belly. I was sick and wretched, and something that had been clear and simple had become tangled and muddied. (So much for my prayer in the little dark church, so much for the summer-scented wind that I had taken for something more than it was. I was glad that I had not wasted good money on that candle!) But when I had forced down the food that I no longer wanted, and remembered to thank the woman for it, I set out for the city, all the same.

Starting early in the day, I got a lift in a market-cart for a good part of the way, and it was not much past noon when I came in through the side arch of the Golden Gate.

The crowds in the Mesé, that runs magnificently from end to end of the city, seemed somewhat thinner than usual; and I wondered why, until I came close to the towering colonnaded walls of the Hippodrome and heard the roar of the crowd within, and then I realized that it must be a chariot-racing day, and half the city had gone to shout for the Blue or the Green. Later, there would be faction-fighting in the streets, there always was, and is, on a race day. But for the moment, it was oddly peaceful.

I turned up one of the side streets just short of the Church of the Holy Wisdom, then into another, passed under the striding arch of a white stone aqueduct, and found myself in a part of the city where I had seldom been before. A man in the doorway of a perfume shop told me which way to go, and so I came to a quiet street running uphill towards a slim pencilling of cypresses clustered about the pinkish dome of a church.

The Street of the Golden Mulberry Tree, said a passer-by; yes, this was it.

But I turned and drifted off again, up one street and down another; sat for a while on the steps of another church, watching the sparrows foraging among the dry horse-dung in the roadway, and listening to a travelling astrologer at one street corner and a seller of fermented mares' milk at another, both crying their wares. And it was early evening when, despite myself, I came back to the Street of the Golden Mulberry Tree, and began slowly to make my way up it towards the last house on the right. The streets were already in shadow, though the upper storeys of the houses still caught the leas of the sunlight, thick as run honey. The last house of all, the House of the Physician, stood tall and narrow above the rest, even in that street of tall and narrow houses. Save for an arched doorway, it showed, like most houses in the city, only a blank wall to the street on the ground-floor and the floor above. One small window above that, and then on the two top storeys, broke out as a plant breaks into flower, into a riot of overhanging windows and delicate traceried balconies set with pots of trailing bright-coloured flowers that spilled over the balustrades. I stood beneath it, with my head tipped far back to look up, as though into the branches of a tree.

It seemed that I had a long journey behind me, and now that it was over, I did not know why I had come. It would be so easy to cross the narrow street to the arched doorway, and knock, and ask to speak with the Lady Alexia. But I could not do it. If I did, she would help me, I knew that; but she would think that I had come with my hand held out because I was down on my luck and hoped that she would think she owed me something for the day I had killed the cheetah. Worse still, I should never be quite sure within myself that it was not true. Next time she went out to the farm, they would tell her that I had been there asking for her; but that would not matter, because by then, I should be somewhere else. Where, I did not know, did not care; but I wouldn't go asking my way in a church again. . . .

How long I stood there, looking up, I do not know. Not very long, I suppose, for the sun was still bright on the upper windows reflecting back the western sky, and the shadows of flower-jars and iron-work tracery were still pencilled on the plastered walls. Once, I thought something moved behind the thick glass of that single lower window; something that could have been the pale blur of a face. But when I looked at it, it was not there.

I was just turning away, when the narrow door opened, and a little old woman, wizened like a last year's walnut, came out. She looked across the street to me, and beckoned. Then, as I did not check, she came pattering after me, catching at my sleeve.

'My mistress bids you to come in.'

I checked then, and stood looking down at her. 'Your mistress?'

'The Lady Alexia. She sent me to bid you—'

'And if I will not come?'

'She says I am to bring you!' said the little old woman, looking fierce enough to drag me bodily up the street. Then she dropped her eyes. 'My mistress bade me to ask you—please to enter, for she would speak with you.'

I hesitated, even then; but in the end, I went with her, across the street, and in at the small deep-set door.

20 Shade on a Dusty Road

Beyond the door was a pillared entrance chamber, with stairs leading up from one side. I looked towards them, guessing that they must lead to the living quarters, and the window where I had glimpsed that flicker of a face behind the glass. But the old woman led me across—I had not noticed how uneven my footsteps sounded until I walked across that beautiful tiled floor—and through an archway on the far side, into a garden court.

A narrow slip of a garden, cool now in the rising shade, set about with roses and oleanders and small trimmed pomegranate bushes in narrow beds, water plashing from a lion's mask on one wall into a sky-reflecting basin. And on the broad rim of the basin sat a girl in a straight dress of some dark stuff fringed with blue, her hair bound up, as the women wear it here in Constantinople, in a scarf of fine striped silk twisted about her head. There was red stain on her mouth, and her eyebrows were pencilled into fine arches of beetle-wing black over the green-painted lids; and in that first moment I would not have known her, save for the yearling gazelle that stood beside her, ears fanned out, dark eyes watching me for any sign of harm.

For a long moment she looked at me in silence, and I at her. And then she said, 'So it *is* you.'

And the instant she spoke, her face became the face of the girl of the wild olive tree.

'The small one has done well,' I said, glancing at the fawn beside her.

She touched its head caressingly, and came a step towards me. 'But not you, I think. What has happened? You have been wounded?'

'In Thrace in the spring,' I said. 'They only turned me loose from hospital two days since.'

'And you came here. How did you know where to find me in the city?'

'I did not know. I was only passing—by chance,' I said quickly. When she was next at the farm, I'd be somewhere else, and it would not matter her knowing that I had gone there looking for her. But not now. Dear God let her not know now!

She came close, looking at me very straightly. 'Not by chance,' she said. 'You stood outside this house a long while, looking up, as though you were waiting. I watched you, because I could not be sure it *was* you, until Anna brought you in.'

I mind setting down my bundle, and rubbing the back of my free hand across my forehead with some idea that that might clear it. I was so tired that I could not think properly. 'I—yes, I did know where to find you—I found out. I just wanted to look at the house before I went away from Miklagard.'

'Away? Where are you going?'

'I don't know. A long way off.'

'You've been a long way already,' she said.'That's country dust on your clothes. You went out to the farm looking for me, and Cloe or Michael told you where to find me. Only then you were afraid, weren't you. Afraid and proud. How dare you be afraid, Jestyn Englishman?'

And at that instant I heard someone else come in through the street door.

'Sit down there,' said the Lady Alexia. 'I will come back.'

I sat down where she bade me, on the rim of the fountain basin, propping my staff beside me. A great wave of weariness was flowing over me; stronger than pride, stronger than fear. What did it matter, after all, if she guessed that I had been looking for her at the farm? What did it matter what she thought about it? I was too tired to care. I remember, as in a kind of cloud, sitting slumped with my arms across my knees, staring at the ground in front of me; and that was all.

The chiming of the water from the mouth of the lion mask

behind me deadened other sounds, and I did not hear her feet nor the sharp hooves of the little gazelle following her, as she went into the house, nor the heavier footsteps that, in a while, came back alone. Only suddenly, I was staring, not at the bare paving-stones, but at a pair of crimson boots; and I looked up, to find a man standing over me—a tall man, stooping a little under his own height, with a dark face that seemed all the darker by contrast with his greying hair and beard, and eyes that looked like a desert Arabs with the sun behind them.

'My daughter tells me that you are Jestyn Englishman of the Varangian Guard, who saved her from the Emperor's hunting cheetah, last year.'

'I am.'

'Truly an unusual Varangian.' The man had an extraordinarily deep voice, with a liquid note at the back of the throat.

'Why?' I said. 'We are no gentle crew, but it is not our custom to stand by and watch a girl mauled by a cheetah when a little thrust with a dagger is all that is needed.'

'True. But not many of you, I think, could or would have brought a living fawn out of its dead dam by something very like the Caesarian operation.'

'I have worked with cattle all my life, till a while back; and for a master who was the best cattle doctor in five manors. It is not the first time that I have done that thing, though I did not know there was a special name for it.'

I had begun to haul myself to my feet again, but he set a hand on my shoulder. 'Bide still. You have walked over far on that leg, for one two days out of hospital.'

So she had told him that, too. I got to my feet all the same; what I knew was coming had to be met standing up, not sitting down.

'Did you think that maybe we needed a cattleman on the farm?'

I looked him in the eyes. 'I suppose so.'

'And Michael told you he could not take on fresh hands without my word, and sent you here?'

'I don't know why I came,' I said. 'I was not going to ask entry.'

'No. My daugher told me you were already on the edge of going, when she sent Anna after you; which would have been a pity, for I have wished sorely for the chance to show you my gratitude.'

'I did not come seeking gratitude,' I said, rather desperately. 'Nor with my hand held out for the payment of a debt.'

'Did Cloe put that into your head? A heart of gold, but a heavy touch.' He smiled, a slow smile that seemed to creak a little, as though it did not come often to his face. 'Jestyn Englishman, you saved for me the one thing in life, save for my work, that means very much to me. When the debt is great enough, there is no means of paying it; one can give only thanks.'

'I accept the thanks,' I said. 'And I'll be on my way.'

'Not so fast.' I found that his hand was still on my shoulder, and his eyes were holding mine so that I would have found it hard to look away if I had wanted to. 'I have done you the justice to believe that you did not come here with your hand held out, seeking payment for my daughter's life. Now do me the justice to believe that I do not offer the charity your over-hot pride will not stomach. You are through with the Varangians and you need work; no shame in that, surely. And presently we will talk of this, but it can wait. First wash off the dust of the journey and then we will eat. Anna will take you to the bath chamber and find you a fresh tunic.'

And so, without knowing quite how it happened, I found myself, an hour later, with the dust of my journey soaked away in hot water, clad in my one spare shirt, and a tunic of Alexius Demetriades' that fitted me none so ill, sitting at supper with the master of the house, at a table set for coolness under the trained fig-tree behind the house.

Alexia served us, helped by Anna—it was a small household of few slaves, I had gathered that already—then sat down with us herself, while Anna scuffled off into the shadows. The gazelle lay like a slender alert dog at her mistress's feet.

It was very peaceful, the pools of lamplight scarce moving on the table, no stir of wind among the broad leaves of the fig-tree overhead. We had just finished with the hard-boiled duck eggs, and were starting on the baked carp which old Anna had set on the table, when the faint sounds of tumult from the direction of the Hippodrome, which had been going on for some time, swelled suddenly louder. Demetriades sighed. 'It begins. I wonder if there is a medic anywhere in this part of the city ever finishes his supper uninterrupted after a chariot race day.'

'Patching up broken heads is a surgeon's work,' said Alexia. 'You only have to refuse to soil your hands with it, and you can go on to the honey-cakes and figs in peace.'

'Patching up broken heads is also healer's work,' Demetriades said. 'I do not believe I would enjoy the honey-cakes and figs.'

And Alexia gave him a sudden glimmer of a smile. 'I am very sure that you would not. Eat your fish, my father; the first of them will be on the doorsill at any moment.'

And sure enough, before the carp was finished, we heard a distant thumping on the street door. And a short while after, Anna came scurrying out. 'It's the Blues and Greens,' she announced, as one who has announced the same thing many times before.

'Does it look bad?' asked Demetriades, already rising from the table.

She shook her head. 'Who's to say? His friends left him on the doorsill—there's a deal of blood.'

'You have taken him into the surgery?'

Alexia had risen also. 'I will come and help—Anna, keep Maia with you.' Then she half-turned back, and looked at me. 'My father's dresser left us a few days ago. And on race nights there are generally more than one knife-wound to be seen to. I can act as my father's dresser, but I would be glad of another man's strength in case of trouble. There is so often trouble. Will you come?'

I got up. 'Surely, I will come.'

I followed her as she followed her father, back into the house and across the entrance chamber to a door behind the stairs. Beyond the door was a square room bright with hanging lamps, a table in the middle, chests and closets round the walls, and on a bench, a man sitting slumped, holding his head as though he were afraid that if he let go it would fall off. Blood ran between his fingers, out of his matted hair, and he looked very like somebody who has been hit by half a brick.

Demetriades went to him, and put a hand over his for a moment, before drawing it away. 'Show me.'

'One of those accursed Greens!' said the man thickly. 'May he rot in Hell!'

Demetriades parted the hair and looked at the jagged wound. 'Aye, aye, a little more to the right, and you might have been rotting in Hell yourself—as it is, there's no great harm done.'

Anna brought hot water in a bowl, and Alexia took it and set it down, then began to help her father, holding the man's head while he clipped away the matted hair and bathed the gash. Clearly she was well used to such work, and at first I did not think there was going to be any need of me at all. Then, as Demetriades was cleaning out the wound with palm spirit, and the man bellowing like a bull calf, there came a second beating on the street door. And another man was hauled in by a couple of friends and dumped all asprawl like a shock of wet barley in the corner. All three of them were dripping drunk, but the two friends departed, after explaining—though indeed it was plain for anyone to see—that he'd taken a knife through his left arm just below the shoulder; and it was the wounded man himself who was spoiling for more trouble.

He took one look across at the fellow with the broken head, saw the draggled blue ribbons he wore knotted round one arm, and lurched to his feet again and started towards him. 'Bastard! Trickster! Those horses were drugged, if ever I've seen drugged horses!' And he was fumbling for the knife in his belt.

It's not easy to handle a wounded man set on murder, if you're not wanting to worsen the wound; but I managed to get hold of him—he was a runt of a man, anyway—and sit him down again without much trouble.

'Look now,' said I, 'you're here to get that hole in your ugly hide mended, not to make more holes in somebody else's.'

And Demetriades, in a tone of quiet amusement, said without looking up from his task, 'That is well spoken. Now cut his sleeve off for me—use his own dagger.' And when I had done as I was bidden, the man glowering and mumbling threats and curses the while, 'So—now clean it up so that I can see what the damage is, when I've done with this one.'

Old Anna had brought more warm water and sponges meanwhile, and I set to work, swabbing away the blood as it oozed from the deep gash.

'Will I die?' the man said, watching the water redden. I was going to say, 'One day, and it might as well be now for all I care; but since you *are* here. . . . But I saw the look in his eyes that he turned on me, and it was the look I had seen in the eyes of cattle I had tended—frightened by pain and strangeness, though they knew nothing of the fear of the unknown that men call the fear of death. So I said, 'All men die, one day, but not this time, if you hold still.'

And I had the wound cleaned up and the bleeding almost stopped by the time Demetriades left the first man having his head bandaged by Alexia, and came across the room to take over.

We tended five men that evening, he and I and the Lady Alexia. One, who had been kicked in the groin and belly, was put into a small inner chamber for the night, since it seemed that there might be some hidden hurt within him; the rest patched up and sent on their way.

I mind when all was over, there was a kind of sigh in the lamp-lit room, like a man sighing when he straightens his back from a hard job of work. I had thought I was tired before, but I had not known how tired I was until that moment. 'I've got blood on your tunic,' I said. 'I am sorry.'

Demetriades smiled his slow grave smile. 'It happens.'

Anna had brought more water, for our own washing, this time.

'Will you come back and finish your supper?' Alexia said.

He shook his head. 'I have notes to write up before I go to my bed, and it grows late.'

Alexia sighed. 'Anna shall bring some soup and a dish of figs up to the study.'

'Bid her bring them in here. I shall bring my work down, and watch for a while.' He glanced toward the inner chamber.

'Very well. Come you then, Jestyn Englishman.'

But I was almost past being hungry. Also I had a feeling of strangeness on me. The evening's work had woken in me things that had been sleeping or almost sleeping, for a long while. Following Thormod, I had become a fighting man; that had been all my life, or so I thought, the Viking way had been my way; now, suddenly, I was another Jestyn, who had once been the best cattle doctor after old Gyrth, in five manors. I needed time to grow used to myself again.

I hesitated. And Demetriades, still drying his hands and forearms, glanced at me and seemed to understand something of all this.

'In a while,' he said. 'I think that after all, Jestyn Englishman and I have a word to speak with each other first.'

And as Alexia left the room, he led the way back into the small inner chamber.

Behind the deep drugged breathing of the man on the narrow cot, it was a very quiet room. One small window, full now of darkness, high on the lime-washed wall above the bed; a light burning crocus-flamed below a plain black wood crucifix. Suddenly I wondered how many men had died in that room, whether any had been born in it. It seemed a place very near to such things.

Demetriades bent over the man, feeling the pulse in the base of his throat, then straightened and turned to me. 'Thank you for your help tonight, you have the healing gift in your hands.'

'If so, it was learned on cattle,' I said.

'No. The skill was learned on cattle; the gift is from God.' He hesitated, his eyes on my face, then seemed to make up his mind. 'An hour—two hours since, I had not thought to say this to you. A few moments ago, I had thought to say it tomorrow when you had slept. Now, it seems to me that this is the time to say it.'

I waited, while the quiet of the room sank into me; and after a moment he went on. 'I have always preferred to have a free man, rather than a slave, for my dresser. A few days since, my dresser, being a free man, left me as a free man may, to better himself with a master who can pay him more than I. I have found no one to take his place, until tonight; now it seems to me possible that I may have done so.'

I looked at him, stupid with weariness, not sure that I had his drift. 'Would you mean—me?'

'If you will take his place. He was a good dresser, it would be a place worth the taking.'

'I learned my skill on cattle,' I reminded him.

'He was a good dresser, *after* I had taught him all his skill— as I will teach you.'

'But—but you know nothing of me.'

'Enough, I think. Maybe one day you will tell me more.' Suddenly he smiled, the light of the lamp below the crucifix making a network of fine lines round his eyes. 'Will you not give it fair trial for a month—say, two months?—at the end of that time, if it does not go well, we will talk further concerning Michael and his need for more help on the farm.'

21 'For you too, there was a Patroclus'

So I became dresser to Alexius Demetriades, in the tall house in the Street of the Golden Mulberry Tree. And after a few days, when I had had time to think, I went back to the small dark church, and bought a candle to burn before the picture of the still-faced Madonna. And I prayed. 'Since I am not damned, receive now my thanks.' I almost prayed, 'But let me not forget in all this, that I am waiting for Anders Herulfson. Let me never forget what is on my forehead.' But I knew that there was no need to trouble God or His Mother with that prayer. While I remembered Thormod in his shallow grave in the Thracian hills, I should remember what I owed to Anders Herulfson; and Thormod was a part of me. . . .

At first, my tasks were to fetch and carry for Demetriades, and clear up after him; follow him with his case of drugs and instruments when he went every morning to the great hospital that was part of the Monastery of St. Sebastian; keep his instruments clean and in order; then, later, grind and prepare the simpler drugs, and hold the edges of a wound while he sutured it. And all the while, I watched what he did and listened to his quiet explanations, learning that these were the signs of a diseased heart and these showed forth a sickness within the ears; that this meant no more than the need for a purge, while this was the beginning of death as yet far off. That this fever should be treated with Oil of Ngai Camphor, and this, with an infused mixture of vervain and yarrow. I worked hard, and I learned, I think, none so ill. And at the end of the first two months, there was no thought in me or in my master, that I should go to help Michael on the farm.

Learning of another kind, I gained also—though it too was needful to the craft of medicine. For Alexia taught me to read and write, in the strange Greek script that was different from what little writing I had ever seen before. Greek translations of the books of Arab physicians, Hunayn ibn Isaak, and Rhazes' *Encyclopaedia of Medicine*. It is sad that so many of our greatest medical books are still translations from the Arabic and Persian—other books also, from her father's library that had nothing to do with the theory and practice of medicine, but were simply for joy, such as the writings of the long dead Greek poet, Homer.

So autumn passed, and winter turned to spring, and the trained fig-tree behind the house broke out into leaf buds that were like jets of green flame. And then it was early summer. And Michael had come in from the farm on his weekly visit with eggs and vegetables and the like; and when he went back in the morning, Alexia would be going with him.

It was one of those evenings when the air is like warm milk against the skin. The last egg-shaped sun-spots dappling through the broad leaves of the fig-tree scarcely moved on the page of the *Iliad* open on the table between us. There was a twittering of young swallows under the eaves high overhead, and the deep boom of bees among the red pomegranate blossom. And suddenly I knew how much I should miss these evenings, tomorrow when Alexia was not here.

And not really meaning to, I looked up from the page and told her so. 'I am little of a scholar, but I shall miss this reading together in the evening.'

'You have enough skill now to practice alone,' she said gravely. 'And I shall be back soon, and to and fro all summer. I cannot leave my father for long at a time.'

'Does he go out to the farm sometimes?' I asked.

'Very seldom. He says he is too busy, and that is true. But—the farm came to him with my mother. I was born out there, and she died. Now, I do not think he can bear to go back often, it hurts him too much.' She began to gentle the ears of the gazelle lying beside her. 'We must go on with the reading, or dusk will find us still here.'

So I went on with the reading. It was the twenty-second book of the *Iliad*, telling of Achilles' vengeance for the death of Patroclus, his friend.

'Achilles saw that Hector's body was completely covered by the fine bronze armour he had taken from the great Patroclus when he killed him, except for an opening at the gullet where the collarbones led over from the shoulders to the neck, the easiest place to kill a man. As Hector charged him, Prince Achilles drove at this spot with his lance, and the point went right through the tender flesh of Hector's neck, though . . .'

Suddenly I could not go on; and I left the sentence unfinished. I mind sitting and rubbing my knee, which was aching, as it still does after an especially hard day's work.

'What is it?' Alexia asked. 'Have you hurt your knee?'

I shook my head. 'Just tired. There was a little girl in the hospital today—we couldn't save her—even your father couldn't save her.'

'Even my father is not God,' she said, with that quietness of hers that had always seemed to me like shade on a hot and dusty road. 'And truly, I was right, the first time I ever saw you—you are a most unlikely Varangian.'

I gave her back look for look. She had an elbow on the table, her long chin cupped in her hand. Her eyes stayed on my face.

'I think that I should never have carried my sword in the Barbarian Guard, but that I followed a friend,' I said. 'Yet it was a good time, and I would not be without the memory of it.'

'And this friend? He is not here in the city?'

'He is dead. In Thrace, at the same time as I got my knee.'

I saw her face flush. 'Oh, I'm sorry, I am so sorry, I should not have asked. I think it's because I am going away tomorrow.'

'Please,' I said. 'I am not minding, not now.' And—I suppose that also was because she was going away tomorrow—I began to tell her—oh, so many things that were nobody's business but mine. About my boyhood and the shore-killing, and how Thormod had bought me for six gold pieces and a wolfskin cloak, in the Dublin Slave Market. Of the homecoming to Sitricstead, and the Blood Feud that we carried down from the north, and the ambush among the Thracian hills.

When I had done, we were silent for a while. Alexia was always a good person to be silent with, like Thormod. And then she closed the book, very gently, and said, 'And so for you, too, there was a Patroclus.'

It must have been about a year went by, and it seemed as though my time with the Varangians was many more years than one behind me. I still saw the faces of men I knew in the streets; but the Varangians were beginning even then to be a People unto themselves. Now, they have made one whole district of the city their own; they have their own church; they form all their bonds of friendship and brotherhood among themselves. It was not yet quite like that, but it was already beginning. If you were one of them, you were of the Tribe, the Family; if you were outside, you were on your own. So the men I passed in the street or found drinking at my elbow in the wine-shop belonged to a different world from mine, and we no longer knew how to talk to each other. We spoke each other's names and made a few falsely hearty noises, and then looked away; always looked away.

I began to make a new friend, here and there, in my new world; and for the rest, I worked. Now Demetriades trusted me to dress a flesh-wound or carry out simple treatments when he was elsewhere, though for the most part my work lay still in fetching and carrying and holding; and acting in general as a kind of spare right hand. More than once I spent the night in the small white room behind the surgery, watching over some sick or injured man.

On the morning of one such night, Demetriades said to me, 'Do you remember, nearly two years ago, I said to you that you had the Healing Gift in your hands, and you told me that what skill you had, you had learned from old Gyrth and the cattle? Now, I have taught you more of skill even than old Gyrth ever knew, and the Gift is still there, grown stronger.'

I stood before him, and waited for what would come next.

'With more training, you could become as skilled in medicine as I am myself.' He smiled. 'Maybe more so. Many's the student who has outrun his master. Every man, I suppose, wishes for a son to follow after him in his craft; and since I have no son, I would gladly give you the training that I would have given him.'

Still I waited. I had known, I think, what he was going to say, yet I was unready, all the same. Part of me cried out 'This is the way for you! Take it and follow it!' But part of me knew that by taking it, I should bind myself, not only to Demetriades but to a whole way of life. I who still had the mark of the Blood Feud on my forehead; who was bound to that before all else.

So I shook my head.

'Why not?' Demetriades asked, after a moment.

'Your last dresser was a free man, and as a free man may, he left to better himself,' I said slowly, remembering the words with care. 'But if he had become your student, he would have ceased to be free. And I must be free. For a time at least, I must be free.' I struggled for the words I needed. 'No, not even free; it is that I am bound by an older bondage.'

'If it is the need to go away for a time—'

'No,' I tried desperately. 'If it were that, I could go, and come back. If I were to take this way you offer, I must needs take it with a whole heart. And that I cannot do, for there is another thing that must always come first with me.'

'Can you not tell me what it is?'

But I could not. I don't know why. I had told Alexia.

'If I may be your dresser still, I will do that, and be glad.'

He looked at me long and searchingly, and then bent his head. 'So be it, If one day you should be free of this "older bondage", come to me and tell me so.'

So I went on being Demetriades' dresser; and the months went by, and neither of us spoke again of my training to become a physician. I did not forget. I longed to accept what he offered, but I could not; not with less than my whole self; and no man can give a whole self to serving life, when the thing that comes first with him is the death of another man.

And more months went by, and an autumn evening came. So many of the things that have turned my life seem to have happened in late summer or early autumn. Rain had brought a dank chill to the air, and it was good to feel the warmth of the freshly-lit brazier in the room above the entrance chamber. There was olive wood on top of the glowing charcoal, burning with a clear blue flame, like a driftwood fire but without the salty sparkle. Alexia and I had returned to our reading together at the day's end; though now we read for the most part simply for a shared pleasure, whenever

there was a little time to spare, as there was this evening, when
Demetriades was out late visiting a patient, and had not bidden
me to go with him.

We heard a beating on the door, and voices below, and Anna's
shuffling footsteps on the stair. She came into the stairway arch,
puffing a little with the hurried climb. 'Jestyn Englishman, there
is a man at the street door asking for you. He will not come in
out of the rain, but bids you to come out to him.'

So I went down the stairs and across the entrance chamber. I
had long ago ceased to notice the unevenness of my own footfall
on the tiled floor. It was blue dusk in the street beyond the open
door. Cold air came in, but no sound save the hushing of the
autumn rain. The man was waiting, a darker shadow in the sodden
dusk. He loomed forward in the doorway, into the fringe of the
lamplight; drenched and ragged, gaunt with a gauntness like something that has strayed after many days out of its grave.

He said, as though he had not quite enough breath for speaking,
'I knew that if you lived, you would wait for me. Has it seemed
long, the waiting for Anders Herulfson?'

22 The End of an Old Bondage

I knew the man in the instant before he spoke; a sudden flash of recognition quicker than sight; and realized in the same splinter of time, that I had no knife on me. The smell of danger should have come to me with Anna's message, but some part of me must have been asleep. . . . The lamplight showed me the flash of his dagger, and I flung myself sideways just in time to hear the blade cut wind past my shoulder.

Behind me, Anna was shrieking like a stuck pig as I went for his dagger hand. I got him by the wrist, trying to twist it backward. For a few moments he fought like a bare sark, like a barrow wight; his left arm was round me, crushing out my breath; while I forced my forearm across his throat, thrusting up his chin with all the strength that was in me. We reeled and trampled to and fro; and then he began to cough, and the knife went spinning from his grasp, and in the same instant he seemed to lose strength and almost crumble. I got my sound leg behind his knees, and hooked his legs from under him, and we crashed down together, with him underneath. If the knife had been within my reach, the thing would have ended then and there, but it had been kicked far across the floor; and I was squatting on my good knee and bending over him, shouting for Anna to stop screaming and bring the lamp. I was hauling him further into the room—he had fallen across the threshold and lay half in the street—but Anna's shrieks had fetched Alexia running, and it was she who brought the lamp, and knelt down at his other side.

He seemed to be nothing but bones and sodden rags, and the lamplight on his face cast great shadows into his eye-sockets and under his jagged cheek-bones; and a little blood and pus, that certainly had nothing to do with my blows, was trickling from the corner of his mouth. His eyes began to open, and he fixed them on my face, those odd eyes, one blue, one grey, burning bright with fever in their discoloured pits.

'I came to—finish the feud,' he said, in that same breathless tone, yet only slurring his words a little. 'But it seems that I've left it—just too late.'

And I saw that he expected me to finish it, and was ready. It would have been easy now to reach the knife. . . .

'We can speak of that later,' I said. And to Alexia, 'We must get him into the night-room, and those wet rags off him, he is sick enough without their help.' But that was the voice of Demetriades' training, and under it, a small cold voice deep within me was saying: 'The Norns have given him into your hands. He will be easy to kill, too easy. Then the old feud will be finished indeed.' And part of me thrust the voice away, and part of me listened.

He was horribly light to carry; and soon enough, he was lying on the cot in the small white-walled room behind the surgery, stripped of his drenched rags and wrapped in blankets.

There was an old scar white under his ribs on the left-hand side, and as I looked at it, I remembered the field armoury in the hills beyond Berea, and Anders saying, 'As good as new, save when something still catches me under the rib—like a bee-sting—when I laugh.' Thormod's dagger must have pierced a lung and done some kind of damage that had not healed through the years. Or maybe it had healed and then something had torn the inner scar-tissue, though the outer scar was slim and silvery as the vein on a poplar leaf. Now, there was some kind of lung fever on him; no doubt as to that. Also he was three parts starved. When Alexia returned from quieting Anna, I asked her for some broth, and between us we managed to get a little down him, though by that time he was not much more than half-conscious again. And when that was done, I set to work to find out if that might be what the mischief was, and how bad.

I had no need to feel for the pulse at the base of the throat, for Anders was so thin that I could see the life beating there, fast, much too fast; I could hear the painful breathing that only half-filled his lungs as though the top of each breath was cut off with a knife. He had been sweating when I put the blankets around him, now he began to shiver; long agonizing shudders that ran through him, shaking the narrow bed; and yet his body when I touched it was as burning hot as ever. And I noticed how, even half-conscious, he lay curved a little to the left as though drawn down by pain in his left side. Demetriades had long since taught me how to listen to the sounds under men's ribs, by tapping with a finger of one hand on a finger of the other spread against the chest wall. I did that now, and all down the left side of Anders' ribs the sound that came back was dull and sodden, instead of the clear drum note that should answer to one's fingers there.

I was too intent on what I was doing, to hear a footstep, and movement beside me, but suddenly Demetriades was there. He bent over Anders, and set a hand on his forehead, then felt the painful knot of life beating at the base of his throat. But he only said, 'Who is he?'

'A man I knew in my days among the Northmen. Anders Herulfson. It is the lung fever.'

Demetriades had his hands on either side of Anders' chest, feeling the difficult breath come and go. 'An old enemy?'

'No,' I said.

'I think, not an old friend—Anna was telling me something concerning a dagger.'

'He was delirious.'

'So, and delirious, just chanced to find his way to this house and ask for you by name?' His hands were moving here and there, testing, probing. 'No, I'll ask no more questions.' He began to tap, the finger of one hand over the finger of the other, as I had been doing, returning again and again to that dull-sounding left side that told of fluid where there should be air, returning to one particular spot in the left side, not far from the little silvery scar.

Anders coughed again, and more blood and pus came out of his mouth, and I wiped it away.

'He has the lung fever,' Demetriades agreed, as though I had just said it, and there had been nothing else in between. 'Do you know why?'

Even now, he did not cease to be the teacher.

'That scar—' I hazarded.

The physician nodded. 'That for the first cause, I should think at least two years ago. Now, a lung abscess. Oh, it may have been lying dormant a long while, many months, but now, a lung abscess. You should not have missed that.'

'I have not yet had so long practice as you in hearing through my fingers,' I said.

'Did you not look at his hands? Look at them now.'

I looked, and saw that the finger-nails that should have been straight, were curved over at the tips, and the part between the base of the nails and the top joints swollen, so that they had a clubbed look. No one knows, though maybe we shall one day, why that happens with a lung abscess. 'I have looked,' I said. 'And I will remember another time.'

Demetriades stood back from the cot, I with him. He must remain here,' he said. 'If he has a chance of life, to move him now even over to the hospital, would destroy it.'

'Has he a chance?'

He was silent a moment, then he said, 'Even Lazarus had that. If we could cause the abscess to burst and drain. . . . We will try linseed poultices, at least they can do no harm, and may ease him somewhat.' He began to turn back his loose sleeves as he spoke.

'Go to your bed, Master,' I said. Indeed he looked as though he might drop himself, with weariness. 'I can handle that.'

He hesitated. 'It is true that you can do as much for him as I can, at this stage.'

Something made me look at Alexia standing in the doorway. It was as though she had called to me in some way that made no sound. Called with her eyes maybe, for they were fixed on me intently enough for that, with a strange questioning in them. She knew all that her father did not, about Anders Herulfson. Just for the moment, our gaze met, and then, as though she was satisfied, she looked away.

Demetriades was giving me my instructions, for the poulticing, for giving him the poppy drink if the restlessness or pain increased, and oil of the dried Indian root the Turks call Altum Koku to cool the fever and help to bring up the evil humours in his chest.

'But if there is any downward change, call me at once,' said the old physician. 'Come, Alexia, there is no more work for you here, at the present time.'

And then I was alone, as I had been time and again in that room with sick or injured men. But this time it was different. This time, the man was Anders Herulfson.

I remember standing and looking down at him, and thinking that he had killed Thormod and now the thing was between him and me. Through all the time since the ambush in the Thracian hills—and surely they had been evil times—he had nursed the thought of killing me, as I waiting here in the city, had nursed the thought of killing him. It could be finished so easily now; a little pressure on the windpipe, and I would feel the life go out, under my hand. And I knew that it was too late; for me as well as for him, it was too late.

I was sick and shaking, and there seemed to be a tight band round my forehead. How long I stood there, I don't know. I found that I had thrust a hand into the breast of my sark, and was clinging to Thormod's piece of amber on its blood-stained thong. I loosed my grip carefully, as though I were loosing somebody else's, finger by finger; and turned and went out to the kitchen quarters to ask Anna for boiling water and to leave the fire made up so that I could boil more as I needed it, through the night.

Then I went back, got a little of the Altum Koku down Anders, and began to make ready the linen cloth and linseed.

The night went on its slow way. Anders was restless, shivering and sweating by turns, muttering of things that made sense to him in the twilight place that he had wandered to, but made none to anyone listening. I kept up the poulticing, rubbed him down with tepid water to cool the fever that was burning him up, wiped away the blood that came when he coughed. It seemed so little, but there was nothing more, save wait, and watch for any change.

And in the darkest hour of the night, a change came. At the time it seemed a wonderful thing. Suddenly he drew a deep breath, deeper than any I had seen him take that night, and coughed up a great mass of blood-stained filth. The poulticing, it seemed, had done its work, and the abscess had burst! Laying him down again—for I had been holding him while the coughing lasted—and cleaning up the mess, I wondered whether I should call my Master. But there was no need, the abscess had burst;

now, if it drained properly, the fever should abate of its own accord; now there was a chance of life for Anders which had not been there before; but in all this, there was no cause to go breaking into Demetriades' much needed rest.

Sure enough, Anders' breathing grew easier, and the fever began to go down almost at once, and not much more than an hour later, turning from measuring out his next draught, I found Anders watching me, eyes bruise-rimmed in skeleton face, but perfectly awake and aware.

'This is an unlikely place and—an unlikely task, to be—finding you in,' he said, low and dry.

'Let you not talk,' I said, almost without thinking. I had said much the same thing to so many sick folk before.

He gave a broken breath of laughter. 'But I want to talk, and I'll do what I want—while I can. It can make—but little difference now.'

'I'd not be so sure,' I said. 'You are better. Drink this—it will loosen your cough and help you clear the filth out of your chest.' And I raised him against my shoulder, and held the Altum Koku to his mouth. He looked at me, and I at him, and for the moment not as enemies. It was as though there was some kind of truce between us. Then he drank, and I laid him down again.

His gaze was still on my face. 'I thought about this—reunion— all the while I was in—the Bulgars' hands. Oh yes, they captured me. I'd not be knowing—why they didn't kill me, save that they— were short of pack animals. . . . So I served as a pack pony among the mountains until—I escaped in the spring. A thunderstorm stampeded the ponies, and—I took my chance. I knew—I'd not likely get another.'

'How did you know I was in Miklagard?'

'I didn't. But with a crushed knee—I reckoned you'd not be on campaign in the mountains—any more. I reckoned if you were —still above ground, the city was the—most likely place to seek you. It's taken me—all summer, but I got here three days ago, and went to—to the Varangian Barracks for word of you. They told me. Old Thunderfist told me—where I should find you—'

'You went to the Varangians? Knowing there might be those among them who saw how Thormod died?'

'Why not? I am changed. I knew there was little chance that— any would recognize me if I did not shout my name.'

'I recognized you,' I said. 'I knew you in the dusk, before you spoke your name.'

He was silent a moment, his eyes still on my face. 'As I would recognize you,' he said at last. 'But then, there is a thing between you and me which is as strong as love.'

By morning, the fever was a good way down, and Anders was sleeping fitfully. 'If the evil humours do not build up again,' Demetriades said, tapping with his fingers and listening once more, 'it seems possible that we shall yet save this man who is not your enemy.'

That day, going about my ordinary work, everything seemed unreal to me. I do not think I killed any of my Master's patients; but half of me was all this while in the narrow white-walled room behind the surgery where Alexia and old Anna were tending Anders Herulfson. Three times during that day, I snatched a moment to see for myself how the thing was going; and the first twice, it was going none so ill, but by evening the fever was mounting again, and when I went to take up my night watch, he was clearly growing weaker. The bursting of the abscess had been only a respite, after all; and the respite was over.

'Maybe one day,' my master said, straightening from the bed, 'we shall find stronger weapons against this sickness. Now, there is little we can do but accept defeat, and give him what peace we can for his dying.' He turned away; and once again I was alone with Anders in the cell-like room with the lamp on the wall throwing the shadow of the crucifix up towards the ceiling.

The night passed much as the first had done, until a little before dawn, Anders roused from his poppy-drink sleep, and came back to himself and began to talk. His voice was so dry and weak that I had to lean close to catch what the said, but the words made sense again. At first it was only that he wanted water, but when I had given him a few sips and laid him down again, he held on to my wrist. 'Did Thormod ever tell you how he and Herulf and I— how the three of us listened to travellers' tales and planned to make our fortunes—see the—Golden City of Miklagard?'

'He told me,' I said.

There was a grim shadow of a smile on his mouth, as I wiped away a trickle of blood. 'He would, of course. . . . We never made

our fortunes, but—three of us have seen the splendours of Miklagard, though not—quite the same three.'

He seemed to doze again for a little while, then he opened his
eyes wide, fixing them full on my face. 'When I missed my stroke,
two nights ago. Is it only two nights ago? I thought that you would
kill me. That was—the way it should be, and—I was ready. Why
did you not?'

'I don't know,' I said.

'You and—the old man with the grey beard—you have fought
to keep the—life in me—as though it mattered, as though the old
wolves had never died in—Svendale. Why, Jestyn?'

'I don't know,' I said again. 'Before your God and mine, Anders,
I don't know.'

'You've gone soft,' he jibed. 'Softer than you always were under
your battle sark.'

'Maybe.'

He was silent again; and I could see that beneath the jibing,
there was some deep trouble in him. After a short while, he said,
'It would have been better if you had ended it, there—in the
doorway. I'm—dying anyway, and now I shall die a straw death—
a cow's death—I never thought I'd come to that. But—maybe
that's why you held your hand. You have a fine vengeance, but—
the dagger would have been cleaner. . . .'

He seemed to be finding it harder to breathe; and I raised him
and held him against my shoulder. The smell of his breath was
like the smell of something already dead. I don't think he believed
it of me, even while he gasped out the bitter words, for he turned
his head on my shoulder, as on the shoulder of a friend. But
whether or no, I saw that there was no time to waste in protesting
my innocence. 'No straw death!' I said. 'Listen! Listen to me,
Anders! Thormod's bee-sting has been slow to kill, but time does
not make a straw death. If ever one of the Viking Kind died of his
wound, taken in war or feud, Anders Herulfson can claim his
company!'

I was speaking loud and fast, trying to reach him before it was
too late; speaking—it was a strange thing—not as the Jestyn I
had become, but as the Jestyn of the *Red Witch* and the Kiev
marshes and the Barbarian Guard. 'Speak my name to Thormod
when you meet him. Tell him both the Old Wolves may sit with

their heads high in Valhalla, for the Killing Time is finished with honour; and both their sons are worthy of them!'

I think he heard me. I hope he did, but he had begun to cough, and a wave of bright blood came out of his mouth.

A great shudder ran through him, and there was a sudden stillness in the room. No more the rasp of painful breathing. And I was once more the Jestyn I had become in the House of the Physician. I felt for his heart, and it was still; and I laid him down. It was near dawn; the rain that had been falling all night had stopped, and the first light was green beyond the small high window. And somewhere in the rain-wet garden, a bird was singing.

I stood looking down at Anders Herulfson, hearing the silence in the room, and the bird singing, and feeling the strange cool emptiness in my heart. I was free of the old feud, the old bondage, and more alone than I had ever been in my life.

The faintest sound behind me made me turn. Alexia stood in the doorway. She stood on the edge of the lamplight, and her hair hung loose and soft on her shoulders. It was the first time I had ever seen it like that; and for the first time, looking at her, I did not think of the dim silver-framed Madonna; only that I needed her and she had come.

She said, 'There will be those among his own kind, who will say that you killed him; and those who will say that it was your right, and your duty.'

And I said, 'I have failed Thormod. But I couldn't kill him.'

'I knew you could not. That is why I left him to you. I did not even tell Father—I knew you could not; but you had to find it out for yourself.'

'How if you had been wrong?'

'Then I think I should have died, too,' Alexia said.

And she came across the narrow room and put up her two hands, and took my face cupped between them, so lightly that I hardly felt the touch of her fingers. 'Listen to that thrush,' she said. 'It is a new day, Jestyn Englishman, a new day.'

I have never been sure whether I did the right thing, or the wrong one, after all. What is wrong in one world is right in another. I failed Thormod, my blood brother; and I do not forget it. But it is all so long ago, now. So long ago. . . .

I went to Demetriades, later that day, and said, 'I am free of the old bondage. Does your offer still hold?'

'It holds,' he said. 'I shall work you as never a master worked his slave, but in the end you will be a better physician than I am.'

It was certainly true, as to the work.

The last light of evening has deepened to a moth-wing dusk, behind the dome of St. Mary of the Barbarians. Alexia is late with the candles this evening. Some crisis in the household, I suppose. But now I hear her feet on the stair, and the light is spilling up before her, yellow as the gorse that will be in full flower now along the English headlands.

I can hear in her footsteps that she is hurrying a little; anxious still? She need not be. I have been sitting here in the twilight, remembering, as old men remember the days when they were young, and the men who were young with them.

But I would not turn back and take another road to another harbouring place. This is where I belong.

Glossary

arval	A funeral 'ale' or feast; as Bride-ale was a wedding feast.
Basil II	963–1025. The greatest of the Macedonian Emperors, known as 'the Bulgar Slayer'. The last of the Bulgarian wars ended in the Byzantine victory of 1014 when 15,000 Bulgarian prisoners were blinded.
Blues and Greens	Rival factions in the chariot-races held at the Hippodrome. So called because of the colour of their caps.
bothy	A hut.
byrnie	A shirt or breast-plate of mail.
Epona the Great Mare	A mother goddess, associated with horses and mules, worshipped by the Celts, and in one form or another by all Horse People, including Roman cavalry.
King Malachy	Maelsechlainn II. 949–1022. King of Ireland.
mazelin	nit-wit.
Mesé	The central street in Constantinople.
Miklagard	The Norse name for Constantinople.
sark	A shirt.
Vladimir	980–1014. Prince of Kiev. His baptism led to the conversion of Russia to Christianity.
wadmal	Coarse wool used for cloaks and the sails of ships.
wankle	Weak in health, delicate.
Wyr Geld	'Man Money': the price of a man's life.

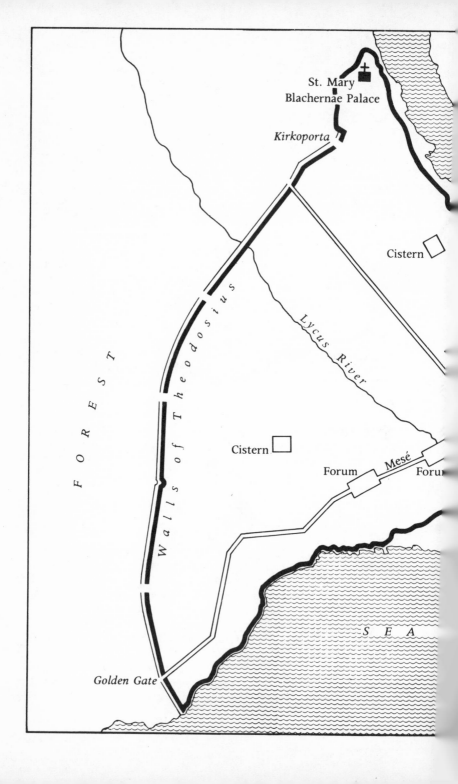

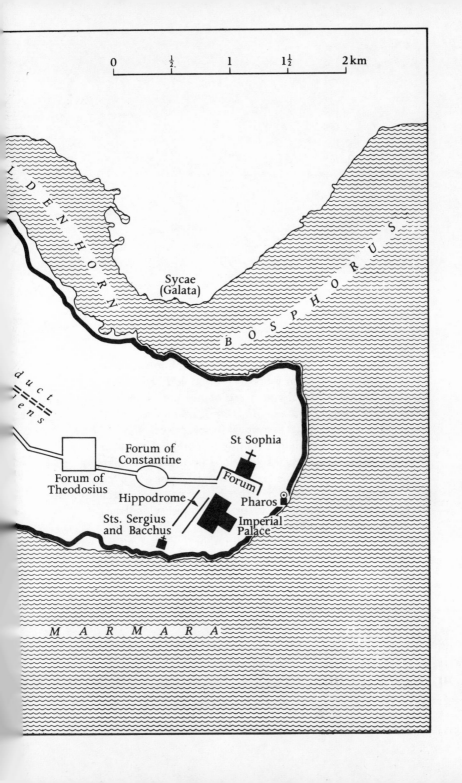

ROSEMARY SUTCLIFF lives in Sussex, England. She is the author of more than twenty books. Her book *The Lantern Bearers* won the Carnegie Medal and many of her books, including *The Mark of the Horse Lord* and *Warrior Scarlet* were ALA Notable Books. *Blood Feud* is her first novel in several years.

Most stories of the Vikings follow their trek over seas and westward to settle the shores of Britain. But the author likes being different, so she chose their route to the Southeast. It led her to such unfamiliar places, she says, that by the end of researching the background she was homesick for the English woodlands.

The theme of the blood feud is common in the Norse sagas. But again the author chose to be different, for the feud she writes about is tragic, in the way a civil war is tragic, because it is between friends.

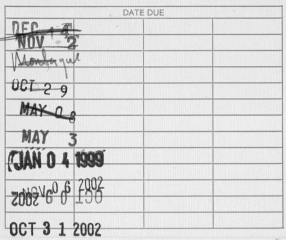